The Good Lover

Steinunn Sigurðardóttir

The Good Lover

Translated from the Icelandic
by Philip Roughton

World Editions

Published in Great Britain in 2016 by World Editions Ltd., London

www.worldeditions.org

First published as *Góði elskhuginn* in Iceland in 2009 by Bjartur, Reykjavik

British Library Cataloguing-in-Publication Data
A catalogue record for this book is available on request from the British
Library

ISBN 978-94-6238-013-4

Typeset in Minion Pro

This book has been translated with financial support from

MIÐSTÖÐ ÍSLENSKRA BÓKMENNTA
ICELANDIC LITERATURE CENTER

Distribution Europe (except the Netherlands and Belgium):
Turnaround Publisher Services, London
Distribution the Netherlands and Belgium: CB, Culemborg,
the Netherlands

This book is dedicated to the writer Málfríður Einarsdóttir
(1899-1983).
A friend—and mentor, in hindsight.

But it is a fact that in every man
(not every woman) there lives a lover.

Joseph Conrad
Chance

A Traveler

Not a dream. Radiant green hills filled the entire horizon—what was once a seabed, the book stated. An hour's hike from the beach that Lotta found for him, according to his preferences: yellow sand, secluded, maybe even remote. And it was very remote, more abandoned than secluded, and more than yellow; that is, golden.

The traveler sat down and gazed at a thousand uprisen hills beneath streaming clouds like Biblical revelations. He took off his shorts when it started pouring rain in the midst of sunshine, fell asleep rain-drenched and woke up dry—stared in amazement at his own naked body on the seabed that was. He had woken to the cries of a cuckoo that leaned toward his toes and fell gravely silent, like a messenger waiting for a signal to commence his delivery.

The sun was gone when he returned to the beach. He sat down on a dune, dug his toes into the golden grains and let his mind wander as he scrutinized the sea that took the color of the sunless sky. There was no one in sight until a man came riding his bicycle along the water's edge. Tomorrow he would do the same, rent a bicycle and pedal thirty kilometers, two trips back and forth on the long mirror between sky and sea.

Around noon he walked to the end of the beach, ate bright red fish in a bamboo hut and drank white wine from the Loire Valley. That something from the Loire Valley should have found its way here! The sun returned and shone full blast over the pitch-black, craggy island on the opposite side of the slender channel. On the way back he amused himself by examining clusters of pebbles that cast shadowy lines on the sand.

He planned to spend the rest of the day taking turns swimming and lying in the sand, regardless of where the sun and clouds were going. In the evening he would sit out on the balcony and watch the dull gleam of the moon sail across the sea. Not move a muscle; eat dinner on the balcony. Let the purl of the waves lull him to sleep. Much later.

On his first visits to distant beaches, he would recall: I'm alone. That was in the past. Yet behind every moment that he existed, alone with himself, especially on the beach, there were moments with kisses and music, during the winter that was, with spring and midsummer, and although they were so thoroughly gone, so long gone, new moments had their origin in them as well as their right to exist.

Ahead there was nothing else to seek; as such, he lived in the present, and anything called the future had nothing to do with him. He didn't hurry, was free from impatience—everything he needed was within reach, here and now. People said that it was good to be close to him, especially his lovers, and that was because he didn't have any particular destination. As a result, he was little inclined to change his travel plans, let alone out of the blue.

Which is why Lotta broke custom and asked a direct question when he called her from the water's edge at dusk and said that he wanted to go to Reykjavík at the first opportunity. She asked: 'What happened?'

A colossal chill hung over the town and in the town on a February morning around the time when people stirred, and coldest of all, the sea itself around the little frost-encrusted island with a few lights lit above the pitch-black beach. The dark blue sea was so off-putting that the traveler driving along the coast felt sorry for the fishes to have to live there and couldn't see how any creature kept itself warm in those depths, no matter how cold its blood was. The traveler knew that a warm-blooded person could live only a short time in the sea beyond the city of his birth. Drowning came quickly—although those who had narrowly escaped that fate claimed it to be peaceful.

A fleet of frost-covered cars, cold through and through, stood waiting for children and adults who were assembling in the vestibules of all the neighborhoods and dressing themselves warmly for the short stretch outside to them. Cold-weather shoes of all sizes were just then ending up on the correct owners, some wide, others too small, pinching unhardened toes and, in the worst cases, turning them permanently crooked.

Low wage earners, along with students, immigrants, and eccentrics, had started to trickle into the bus shelters, hapless folk in other respects than that something called in literature 'dawn's gleam' was being born in the east; here it was a lighter streak of gray within a universal grayness. These people were cold, no matter how warmly they dressed, and some weren't even dressed well enough. The worst-off held the hands of icy blue children, while the children were even worse off than the ones holding their hands.

In the swimming pools this winter morning were unnaturally thin, sinewy, shriveled folk over sixty, folk who walked barefooted on the brittle ice on the banks of the pools without batting an eyelid; excessively healthy people who suffered neither sore throats nor heart murmurs, but would still cost society and themselves large sums of money by living until no less than ninety, and some of them even longer.

Over these people and over the cold in the town and the sea loomed a radiant, early-morning full moon, like the exposed offspring of the sun, giving a false promise of warmth that could never shine from it, not on this town, this sea, nowhere.

The traveler watched the taxi drive off and lingered in the starbright calm outside his accommodation. The red wooden house catty-corner from him was one of the few left belonging to the Skuggi neighborhood of old. Otherwise they had all but disappeared, or had been blocked by other buildings, like his old corner house that stood in invisible silence behind a cluster of highrises.

He listened closely, as if the music from the house would come to life if he only listened; Jussi Björling singing about the woman he loved, but hopelessly; Ástamama and the actor with the bass voice belting out the waltz from *Der Rosenkavalier*: *Ohne mich, ohne mich, jeder Tag dir zu lang ... Mit mir, mit mir keine Nacht dir zu lang ...*

A row of jagged icicles hung threateningly over the door of the red house. The traveler had always been afraid of icicles. People had been killed by icicles falling onto their heads. Later he discovered that an icicle is the perfect murder weapon. It melts.

He was considering moving when the door of the red house

opened and a young man with bronze-colored hair rushed down the stairs. As the door slammed shut, an icicle fell and shattered on the landing. The one whom it nearly struck didn't look over his shoulder at the crash, and continued his dash toward the sea.

The traveler ignored the elevator and darted straight up the stairs like a salmon on its journey home. Panting and puffing, he opened the door to the penthouse and stood frozen in the doorway when the gas station appeared, a black sea and iron-gray Mount Esja beneath a low moon.

He collapsed onto a white leather chair by the window. His heartbeat returned slowly to normal as he took in the view behind the shadow of the kiss on the girl's face the evening that the present took shape and transformed into the future.

It was in fact February. A whole month and more he had gotten to be near the girl, who smiled either wonderfully or mischievously. He still knew her smiles by heart after all those years: the wonderful smile that dwindled slowly and left a little mark on her face long after it had disappeared—and the mischievous smile that came and went so quickly that one needed to be very alert to catch it.

It was stormy that night after the movie. They fought against the wind and spray of the waves on Skúlagata, had hot dogs and Cokes at the gas station, and she came home with him and said something sounding like 'Yes' after the kiss. Now, that jumping-off point for the future appeared to him like a hallucination in the moonlight.

When he finally got up, stiff to his toes, he realized that the door behind him was open and his suitcase was in the corridor. Leaving behind evidence like that was so unlike him. Astonished, even slightly horrified, he corrected his blunder.

The penthouse apartment was as it should be. Clean in style and spacious. A high ceiling, white walls, a dark parquet floor.

Few pieces of furniture, but elegant. An espresso machine that he would have chosen himself. No unsightly clutter. But one thing was lacking. The roses. Not good enough. The price of the apartment demanded that it stand up to the smallest detail. The roses were actually the main point. He was going to call Lotta to get her to set this straight, but of course it was night in North America.

There was no lack of things to choose from in the refrigerator. A starving man eyed the skyr and cream, smoked lamb, and Grandma's Flatbread. Too worn out to do anything, he gulped down Icelandic tap water and collapsed crosswise onto the two-meter-wide bed covered with a dark blue cashmere blanket.

When his mind cleared after long, confused dreams with melodies from Nino Rota, he was thoroughly irritated at his own behavior. He had broken rule number one: had travelled to this country without informing his sister Fríða and niece Ásta. He was ill-prepared for Frosttown and would have to buy himself some warm outerwear if he planned on going to the cemetery with roses for the grave of Ástamama.

The traveler was in such a state that he had to focus hard to open his suitcase and hang up his trousers and jacket, take out his black pajamas and lay them on the bed. He'd slept in underpants and a t-shirt, something that he couldn't recall ever having done; he'd been a pajamas-boy all his life.

Despite his nagging hunger, he had no interest in the Icelandic delicacies. He wanted a petrol-station hot dog and Coke, plain and simple. A crazy idea that he prepared to carry out by first putting on two pairs of underpants, two pairs of socks, a short-sleeved shirt, a paper-thin sweater.

When he came outside, he expected to see suspicious characters lurking about, and he looked in the direction of the old icicle house. But there was no one out in the February darkness

16

except for a tramp who shouted *Ho!* like someone lost on a foggy heath.

The hot dog proved to be problematic for the traveler, because there were now all sorts of bacon-wrapped hot dogs and grilled hot dogs to choose from, with potato salad, shrimp salad. He stuck to a good old regular hot dog with everything on it but raw onions, and a small bottle of Coke. It tasted exactly like it did in the old days, and he dimly envisaged his girl coming there sometimes to relive that stormy evening of long ago.

He was on his way out when he saw the roses. Maybe they would suffice, rather than nothing at all, for a man who'd been falsely promised real flowers in his overpriced accommodation. The white roses were the best of the lot, but a bit too funereal, so he chose yellow ones.

A young man with bronze-colored hair came in as he was paying. The one who lived in a house full of perfect murder weapons but didn't know how to guard against them. And what was he doing at the gas station? Sizing up a traveler in a Dior overcoat?

The traveler wanted to be certain that he wouldn't be followed to his apartment. Which meant only one thing: he had to take a taxi. He would have to figure out later how to explain the absurdity of being driven the distance of several buildings. Maybe make up a leg injury?

The cashier didn't understand Icelandic and ordered the taxi in English. That was in keeping with the new Reykjavík. Urban sprawl had affected everything: inordinate intersections in town, gigantic developments that laid their shadowy paws over the wooden houses. As if to cover over what once was, the past and smallness. The language itself had become too small.

While waiting for the taxi, the traveler contemplated the

roses. One of them stood out; it had the biggest bulb and the straightest stem. He drew it closer; dead straight, with beautiful petals. It was beauty in all its glory. This would be a privileged rose, which he would keep when he threw away the others.

The driver said 'Yes' unusually loudly when the passenger gave him the address on Seltjarnarnes: Silfurströnd 3. That immense 'Yes' resounded like a heavy sentence of doom in the ears of the man who had unwittingly announced the world's most absurd destination.

It had never crossed his mind to approach her. Not even by looking her up in the phone book, calling just to hear her voice before hanging up. Why should he have tried as much as that? She was lost forever. He understood that perfectly when she said what she did, staring at the Swiss roll that he'd made for her. It was irrevocable, and he had left the table hurriedly so that she could go her way.

As soon as he no longer heard her footsteps on the street, he knew that life had become just a memory; he would become a man who had nothing to expect of the future. Futureless man; that was the term for him, and he could not rid himself of the still-life image of a kitchen table set with the finest service and a half-eaten slice of Swiss roll.

When the taxi stopped at number three he said: Oh, it was the next house, and then he paid the driver and stepped out. He kept the one true rose and left the rest of the bouquet in the back seat. A perfect place to get rid of it. Either the next passenger would take it, or the driver himself.

The air on Seltjarnarnes was perfectly still, and the sky above Silfurströnd cloudless. The moon and stars were out, high up in the sky and in the dark sea. The sidewalk was frosty, and he stood there bare-handed, holding a rose—as if he were about to hand it to someone.

He waited until the taxi had driven out of sight before taking any steps toward her house. A two-story house, so strictly funkis that he named it monkish, and earned top points from his girlfriend for it. Those who had had it built, her parents, were, on the other hand, not quite in tune with its character, and decorated it with flowered curtains and carved pine furniture. Those oversights were gone now. Curtains as if the architect had chosen them himself (perhaps he had done so), sofa and floorlamp as if cemented to the floor. The painting as if it were nailed to the wall. He guessed it was by Svavar Guðnason.

Last time (in his former life!), he saw the house in the dazzling brightness that unveiled and exaggerated its good attributes, but now it turned out that darkness suited this house well; it was a nocturnal house. The darkness softened the austere simplicity of its form, and the garden landscape, with spotlit pine trees here and small hills there, formed a vivid contrast to the rectangular concrete and glass.

A woman wearing dark-blue pajamas appeared behind the oblong living-room window. The venetian blinds slowly descended. And the woman's shadow switched off the lamp and disappeared.

He saw at once that little had changed. The same powerful, yet soft gait. Her hairstyle the same: short, bangs, parted in the middle (a Louise Brooks bob). She hadn't gained much weight; only five kilos, maybe, and it suited her face better—her high cheekbones and aquiline nose. She was perhaps even more beautiful now than as a young woman. The man on the street was as proud of her new beauty, as if he himself had added color and glow to a female image that had been radiant enough already.

He was going to wait for her to switch on a light in the bedroom. He knew where it was; knew the house like the back of his hand after the one and only time he'd been there. At the time, she had just moved from Grundarstígur. It was a sunny evening in July, and it was true that he'd been in the same house and garden, in this life, with the woman in blue pajamas. She had settled there, in the house of her parents, where they had spent an evening together and gazed at the ocean, which was still as it had been and not infinite, since it ended on the beach in front of this house, on the same rocks as then.

The light switched on in the bedroom, and he threw the rose onto the sidewalk as he walked. Marble! How gauche. Something that the man of the house had come up with, no doubt. His girlfriend had had such precise taste that he used to tease her about having absolute vision. Now she would enjoy the sight of a frosty rose sculptured on the marble when she looked out in the morning.

He crossed the street and sat down on a bench in the bus shelter across from the house. His heart hadn't beaten any faster when she appeared at the window. This is what he had come halfway across the world to see—why should his heartbeat have sped up?

The light in the bedroom went out; it was completely dark in the house, but the outside lights were on and amplified the snow-white pine that reached out to him over the edge of the garden of number five. Now the woman in number three was pulling a duvet over herself. She was lying on her side, because she always slept on her side, finding it the most comfortable position, and if she was still quick to slumber, as she had been most often in her youth, she might be in dreamland before he rounded the corner.

The traveler, who was usually in no hurry, wanted nothing more than to sit in that bus shelter until the break of day, but the cold drove him to his feet. He was going to order a taxi, but could remember neither the number of the taxi service nor that of Icelandic directory assistance. A taxi certainly wouldn't just show up by chance, no more here than at the end of the world.

He set his course toward a concrete block that was perhaps a shopping mall. Hopefully there he could find a pay phone, a phone book, and a taxi. He ran the last few meters, because his unprotected ears stung fiercely, but it was more like heading for the summit of a mountain, when the destination is always farther than it seems.

In the end, his goal became The Yellow Sheep, a shopping-mall bar. He went in, despite everything in him protesting. No matter how desperate the situation. The Yellow Sheep. To be caught dead anywhere near such tastelessness! The Black Sheep, fine, or even The Shorn Sheep; but this! Yellow! How could a sheep be yellow?

The traveler went and waited at the bar, as he normally would, but it mattered little, because the bartender was busy. That is, he had his back turned to his customer and was fiddling with something; hard to say what.

The traveler had to blow his nose and did so, not very loudly, but enough to startle the bartender and make him turn around.

'Good evening,' said the bartender.

'Good evening,' said the traveler, carefully tucking his handkerchief into his breast pocket.

'Sorry I didn't see you,' said the bartender respectfully. To his shores had drifted a long-awaited real customer, who knew how to handle a hanky.

'That's okay,' said the traveler, asking himself when it became possible to see someone with the back of one's head.

'What can I do for you?'

'Whiskey, a double.'

The bartender pointed at one bottle and another, and the traveler was surprised at the impressive assortment. There was even a sixteen-year-old, first-rate whiskey of the same sort he usually kept in his wine cabinet out west on Long Island and down south in France.

He ordered that one, and paid a third of the price of the entire bottle, four thousand krónur. Such overpricing made his blood boil; just like other people with money, he insisted on paying the correct price for things. It wasn't about stinginess, but what was fair and right. The golden ratio—between the quality of the product and the price put on it.

The bartender served using all the tricks of his trade, with shrewd politeness. Instead of asking whether his customer would like his whiskey with water or on the rocks, he brought him a pitcher of water, a glass of water, and ice in a bowl. The whiskey glass was the right one, as was the water glass. A bartender of his cut would have been at home in a high-end bar for the elite, if he wasn't a bit too fond of his drink.

The traveler shivered from the cold and had to make an effort not to spill his drink as he raised it to his lips. The bartender watched, and naturally, drew his own conclusion based on his expertise. An alcoholic, in such bad condition that he hadn't yet managed to drink off his tremors despite the lateness of the evening.

This traveler was always picky about seating at a bar or restaurant. Now he looked around for the perfect place, as far as possible from two older men who sat together at a table, shrouded in a cloud of their own smoke and unadulterated silence.

He was about to walk across the room, whiskey glass in one hand and the glass of water in the other, when the song began to play. He quickly put down the glasses and stood there.

Only in a dream do we share the same road ...

The waltz by Lilja Jóns that was a hit when he was little. A song that wouldn't have come into existence had not a little boy once gotten some nonsense in his head.

The thing was that Kalli, his mother's little boy, heard the term 'tuneless' at his friend's house. He didn't fully understand it, but he thought it such an awful word that it literally bewildered him, and he ran off alone to Hljómskálagarður Park and who else knows where. Eventually, he came to the conclusion that the entire world was tuneless. All of its tunes had been used up, and no new ones could be made anymore.

A few days passed in the tuneless world and Kalli seemed so distraught that his mother asked: 'Is something wrong?'

She had come to tuck him in and say goodnight. He wanted to pull his duvet over his mouth, bear up, but he couldn't. Tears welled in his eyes and he whimpered: 'Are all the tunes used up?'

'Wait a minute, Kallikalli. Used up, how?'

'Well, you see, so terribly many tunes and songs have already been made that the world has run out. It's tuneless.'

That evening they went to bed late. Ástamama explained that there were endless possibilities for writing new tunes, new songs. That numerous new songs were being written every day, in every single country in the world, including Iceland.

'Even I can make up a song,' she said; 'just listen.'

And Kalli listened and Ástamama spun up a song about Kalli Tyke.

I always wanted my own little boy,
and here he is, Kalli Tyke.

Now that she'd started, she continued writing songs, first for her Kalli and her Fríða. Then she changed into the singer-songwriter Lilja Jóns, who had her big breakthrough with one of her original songs:

Only in a dream do we share the same road.

How proud he was of his mom when they went to the Performing Rights Society (PRS) building on Laufásvegur to pick up a check, and a nasal-voiced composer who looked lika a mad scientist praised her to the skies for her glorious waltz with its dreamy lyrics.

'An original and catchy melody,' he said, and was so elated about having such an excellent opportunity to compliment a seamstress for her musical talent that he gave her a kiss on the cheek. And her singing was fabulous. 'Particularly fine intonation,' he added weightily, through his nose.

The two terms, *PRS* and *intonation*, settled into Kalli's consciousness like parts of magic spells and became guiding lights in his life. He would have loved to say that he earned his livelihood from PRS payments, and that music is what kept his nose to the grindstone. With a special emphasis on singing and perfect intonation.

As the song was drawing to a close, the smokers stood up and started dancing, elegant and bony, until Ástamama's voice trailed off:

... only for a moment in a dream ...

'They're gay,' said a woman who'd suddenly appeared at the bar, from no visible direction, or audible one either.

'Good dancers,' said the traveler, as he watched them take their seats again, hand-in-hand.

Jón used to be a dance teacher. Biffi is deaf. They were one of the very first gay couples in town. To have come out of the closet, if you could call it that. They should open a museum in their honor. Just a little one.

He wouldn't have recognized him again: Jón with his black

mane and grand mannerisms, who came to Ástamama to chat and have clothes tailored for him. And maybe he wouldn't have remembered him, either, except that one day when Jón arrived, an eleven-year-old girl had just gone down the stairs. He had stood there like an idiot in the kitchen doorway, holding a glass of milk and a cookie, and the guest had said mischievously: *Bon appetit.*

'And were have we come from?' asked the woman.

'I don't know about "we,"' said the traveler, 'but I just came from a walk.'

'It's a nice place for walks,' said the woman. 'In the sea air. And with Snæfellsjökull Glacier practically at your doorstep.'

'I'd forgotten about that.'

'How could you forget Snæfellsjökull? You must live abroad. Yes, you live abroad. You have an accent.'

He had an accent? He, who did his utmost to speak perfect Icelandic on those rare occasions when he had the chance, he who had done all he could to maintain his beloved mother tongue, listening to Icelandic readings in the car, including the scholar Einar Ólafur Sveinsson reading *Njál's Saga.* That he had an accent was hard for him to swallow.

'Well,' he said. 'I have no interest in sailing accent-free under false pretences and pretending that I'm Icelandic.'

'Where are you from, then? German American, or American German. Is your mother American?'

'The other way around. My dad was American.'

He hoped that she would leave, so that he could be alone with his expensive whiskey and the image of a woman lowering blinds over a window. But this person wasn't budging.

Who was she, anyway? Not young. Not old. Not beautiful. Not ugly. Not drunk, at least not very. Far from being sober, though. She was wearing a well-tailored felt jacket with a high-quality wool scarf, but both in obscure colors that he couldn't put his finger on. Rust-red? Greyish green? Her demeanor was like the colors: not all there. Her voice was flat and slightly whiny.

And her questions were importunate and personal. Now she came to the crux of the matter, with an accusatory tone in her voice:

'So there's absolutely no Icelandic blood in you?'

'Not a drop. Sorry.'

'Where did you learn such good Icelandic, then?'

'My dad was working in Iceland, so I used to stay here for long periods of time when I was a kid. My mother was particularly good in Icelandic. She read a huge amount of Icelandic literature and was even personally acquainted with Halldór Laxness.'

'You're lying,' said the woman, who was now starting to sound as if she were the one under interrogation.

'It's really not that unbelievable,' said the traveler, as soon as he noticed that he'd turned into a massive liar. The man who had never told a lie, you might say, unless to a lover, of course, ever since he was a child telling nonsense-stories.

'I really would have liked to have known Halldór Laxness,' said the woman, with a light snort.

'There's no need to know an author personally. You get to know him best by reading his books. You see the person clearly by having nothing but his words before you. No annoying tone of voice, no attitude covering over the words, or laying emphasis on them.'

The traveler said this decisively, as if he were at the podium with his high-school Debate Club—and from that stage, he had melted more than one unhardened female schoolmate's heart without even noticing it. There was only one heart that concerned him.

'I think that no one covers himself more than someone who

26

writes. He drinks in the techniques used to cover himself. With his mother's milk. His words are a cover-up, not an exposure. Artists and composers can't camouflage themselves the way a writer can. Their art is naked, it's straightforward. Words are evasive. In his works, the writer appears as an x-rayed mummy. And an x-rayed mummy can't be understood. Except perhaps by a highly-trained specialist.'

The alien had spoken. The traveler stared at her, dumbfounded. It was time to get out of there.

Out, away, one, two, three, he said to himself, but his will was weakened by the chronological jumble of green sea-hills and a gas station and a woman who appeared at the window after seventeen years and transformed into a shadow. He stood there as if nailed to the floor and heard himself say: 'What can I get you?'

'Same as you're having, thanks,' said the woman sluggishly.

He ordered more of the same and forked over eight thousand krónur. This was a man who always paid in cash, if possible, and Lotta usually made sure that he could. This time, however, he had had to use the ATM at the airport in Keflavík. It was vulgar and awkward, like buying condoms in public. A money-man waving around a wad of cash.

'Outstanding whiskey,' said the woman, as if she were on the verge of passing out.

'Great that they have this type here.'

'Lúter Indriði is the best bartender in town. We're related.'

She kept going, in a half-whisper, as if she were at that stage when strangers become the greatest of confidantes. 'His full name is Hreinn Lúter Indriði, but he just calls himself Lúter, except in writing, when it's H. Lúter Indriði. H comes before L in the alphabet. Which can often come in handy.'

H. Lúter Indriði kept himself quietly occupied in the shadowy world behind the bar. The best bartender in town never addresses customers first, even if they're related. The best bartender in town doesn't involve himself in a meaningful conversation that two strangers have struck up on their own at the bar.

The traveler felt weak at the knees and leaned up against the bar, as if overcome with drink. Rather than being caught in such an unglamorous pose, he asked if they shouldn't perhaps sit down.

'By all means.'

She went first, taking a seat at a corner table farthest away from the two smoking men. On the table were two candles and two roses. The bartender's generosity in overdrive. The traveler glared at the flowers; he couldn't deny that he had deliberately thrown a rose onto the sidewalk tonight. What would the woman in the house say in the morning when she came across a flower lying there; what would this Ingi Bói or whatever his name was say if he found it before her? Luckily, they didn't have a child who might be startled by finding a three-dimensional frost rose on the pavement in front of the house as he was going to school.

The woman had stood up and walked off. He thought she might be leaving because he'd been so rude not to say anything when they sat down, but she returned holding a pitcher of water and two glasses. The customer, serving? What had happened to the town's best, H. Lúter Indriði?

The traveler hadn't noticed anyone enter the bar, but suddenly a newcomer was there: a man holding a bouquet of roses. Was it in fashion now in Iceland to sell roses at bars?

The man with the roses glanced around, before heading straight across the room and holding out the bouquet to the traveler: 'You left these in the car when I drove you to Silfurströnd 3 earlier. Here you go.'

'Thanks.'

'I'd certainly appreciate it if passengers wouldn't always be leaving their crap on my back seat.'

'May I offer you a reward?'

'Goodness, no,' said the taxi driver on his way out.

'Bye, Gummi,' said the woman, and he returned her farewell.

'Bye, Gummi,' said H. Lúter Indriði from the dark nook behind the bar.

'Is he a celebrity here on Seltjarnarnes, this Gummi?' asked the traveler.

'Everyone is, here on the peninsula,' said the woman. 'He's also a neighbor of mine.'

'Where do you live?'

'Silfurströnd 5. What brought you there?'

'I felt like going for a drive by the sea, but I thought it seemed a bit aimless just driving around. That's why I gave him an address. That specific one was just a coincidence.'

'I'll tell that to Una,' said the woman, making a noise that was supposed to be laughter but sounded like a low growl. Like a tired dog had heard something funny and really wanted to laugh.

'Isn't that unnecessary?'

'Yes, it's unnecessary. Nothing gets past Una.'

The man who loved Una said nothing, but repeated this sentence in his mind: Nothing gets past Una.

'Are you married?' asked the woman.

'I'm divorced.'

'What was her nationality?'

'German.'

'They're often first-rate women. The German women who came to Iceland after the war were stocky women who toiled away like Vikings.'

'She's a hard worker, for sure, but is far from being stocky.'

How utterly unthinkable it would have been to have a wife,

let alone a stocky one. He wouldn't even have had a stocky woman as a lover. That was the word he used for the women in his life. Never 'sex partner,' never 'one-night stand,' but *lover*, even if it had nothing to do with love. It was a question of grounding. The closest he would ever get to tangible love.

'Do you have children?'

'No children.'

'What about you? Do you have any children?'

'No. That was a risk I couldn't take. I was determined even at a young age not to have children. There are so many things that can go wrong with a child. And then your life is ruined. I'm immensely relieved not to have a child. Even though I love children. And I understand children. They can tell. They come to me.'

'Children are a tribe I know little about. Except that they're a nuisance on long-distance flights.'

'You're missing out on a lot, knowing so little about children.'

'That's the definition of life—missing out on a lot.'

'Some people gain a lot in place of missing out on a lot. Others gain less than nothing by missing out on a lot. You must be in the group that gains a lot in place of missing out on a lot.'

The traveler wondered if the same could be said about him and his houses, his travels and delightful lovers, plus abundant luxury; that he'd gained a lot in place of missing out on a lot. Una with her eyes that nothing got past. Una, who was sleeping in her house by the sea, on the peninsula where he'd drifted like flotsam onto the shoreline. No, wasn't it more a case of having gained a great deal instead of a lot? Quantity instead of quality?

'What about yourself?'

'It's hard to say. At least I don't have to worry about money. I go swimming in the mornings in the best pool in the country;

it's wonderful, and I spend a lot of time in the steam bath.'

The traveler nearly laughed out loud. This steam-bath woman definitely had an overall diluted look: her eyes, hair, the color of her skin. Almost as if she were missing a color gene. But she certainly was sharp.

When it came to a lover, he never gave any thought as to whether she was sharp or stupid. He wanted her to be easy to talk to, and she mustn't have an ugly voice. She had to have a good sense of humor, or appreciate good humor even if she didn't have it herself. She didn't have to be a beauty, but she had to be elegant. Flawless. And slim, of course.

Those were his standards, but unfortunately, he had a weakness for women who were on the plumper side; women who were slightly fat. He thought this bordered on weirdness, and he almost always chose thin lovers. When he indulged himself with plumper women, he found it gave him a great deal more pleasure. The last one wasn't less than seventy-five kilos, which was actually outrageous. She wasn't even flawless, what with the varicose veins on her calves.

And now it so happened that he'd met this far-too-over-weight woman five times, despite having set himself the goal of meeting no woman more than three times. Was he becoming old and soft? After his one time with Doreen Ash, the system-wrecker. Could it be coincidence, how much the number of lovers he had was reduced following his time with her? Less than one a month for the past three years.

Old and soft. Or simply dazed by the evening's soup of coincidences.

'How did he track me down with the bouquet, that taxi driver Gummi?'

'There's really only one place to go to.'

'You mean he just knew I was here?'

'He knows where everyone is. He has telepathic abilities.

31

Clairvoyant, through and through.'

'Is that epidemic here on the peninsula? Una as well?'

'I didn't say that. I said that nothing gets by her.'

'What about you?'

'I've seen a few things. But I keep them to myself.'

'Did you see me earlier this evening, maybe?'

'Of course I saw you, outside Una's house. You threw a yellow rose onto the sidewalk outside her house.'

'How do you know it was yellow, and that it was a rose?'

'I checked.'

'Are you saying you followed me here?'

'There was no need to follow you. You don't need to be clairvoyant to figure out people's movements. It's so obvious that you've been living abroad that it can be seen in the dark. Of course you wouldn't have remembered the taxi service's number. So you couldn't have gone anywhere but here. It's too cold to walk downtown, and you're not wearing a hat.'

The traveler was about to ask the woman if she'd read a bit too much Sherlock Holmes, but instead he said: 'Are you a regular here?'

'I pop in every now and then. Lúter Indriði and I are cousins. He used to work at Le Meurice in Paris, which caters only to the cream of the crop. It's been three years since he came home. He's got problems with alcohol.'

'He's in the best job, then, for tackling his problem every night.'

'Cousin Lúter doesn't feel well. He's becoming dangerously depressed. Alcohol is poison for such people. And naturally, drinking makes people depressed. Speaking for myself, if I'm feeling worse than usual, alcohol is the first thing I cut out. Then I cut out coffee. If that doesn't do the trick, I go to the steam bath every morning and evening. It's so incomparably cleansing.'

You couldn't argue that the woman wasn't clean. This

traveler was competent to judge, because he had a particularly sensitive sense of smell. Other people's odors never escaped him: soap, sweat, perfume, cleanliness, uncleanliness, general or particular—but he couldn't catch even a whiff of shampoo from this woman. Even less that her breath smelled of anything. If he'd been asked what people were odorless, he would have said no one. Except for ghosts. Is that what she was? A revenant from the house next door to Una's? A sending? And who had sent it?

The traveler wanted to turn the conversation to sendings, but couldn't come up with a good way to do so, and instead asked personal questions of the sort he'd trained himself to avoid. 'Do you live alone?' he asked.

'I live by myself in a two-story building. I don't even have a cat. Just a goldfish. A goldfish isn't much company, you see. A cat would be decent company if it were a standout cat, but a goldfish is really just a non-entity. I read a lot, but you can't read more than seven hours a day, which leaves a lot of hours. I suffer debilitating neuritis, and don't see many other people besides Una and Lúter. They're incredibly kind to me. People who don't have children are often very kind to others. People who have children don't have any kindness left for others.'

'I'm sure you could find yourself some company if you really wanted.'

'Yes, I know. Sure I could. But people are so demanding. Some friends call you after midnight. I once had a friend like that. It just doesn't work. I'm usually in bed by ten.'

'You're past your bedtime tonight.'

'Every now and then I can't sleep, so I stare out the window. And you came walking in through the dark.'

'Staring out the window in the dark. What for?'

'You would understand it if you were me. There's so much in

the February darkness. It's actually darker than in December, and there's something cozy about it, because you know it's going to start getting lighter soon. By April, it's bright and shiny, and there's just one month between February and April.'

'I remember that.'

'The months when you and Una were getting to know each other.'

'Me and Una?'

'The one the rose is intended for.'

'It wasn't intended. My hands were so frozen that I had to drop it.'

'She'll find it in the morning. She'll know who it's from.'

'What do want from me?'

'Una told me about you.'

He hadn't intended to finish his drink. Now he drained his glass.

'I've had enough,' he said to his drinking partner. 'If you'll excuse me.'

'Sure.'

'Thanks for the chat,' he said, and stood up.

'Should I order you a taxi?' asked H. Lúter Indriði, having had even more to drink.

'You think you can manage it?' the traveler heard himself say, as if he were someone else. A German American, or American German. He wasn't used to talking to people like that, least of all wait staff. In restaurants, he could seem almost apologetic when ordering a specific dish or wine. Or almost as if he were asking whether he was doing the right thing. Whether it was all right for him to be there in the first place. If it turned out that the wine he ordered was off, he acted is if it were his own fault when he let the waiter know. More than one lover had mentioned this. Namely, the bossy women. The ones he generally managed to avoid. Luckily.

'No problem,' said H. Lúter Indriði, before ordering a taxi with consummate style.

'Whose idea was it to call this bar The Yellow Sheep?' asked the traveler.

'It was just an idea I had. I can't bear bars with cool names. Bars should have corny names. Preferably as pitiful as possible.'

'Well, you succeeded.'

'Yes, don't you think? There's no tackier name than The Yellow Sheep. And it brings in customers. People want to get hammered at The Yellow Sheep—you know, follow the herd.'

'You should have had been awarded Grand Prize for Tackiness.'

'I was.'

The door to The Yellow Sheep opened. A gust of wind blew out two candles.

The shoulders of the man who entered were hunched up to his ears and his head was lowered, as a defense against the weather, and he looked as if he had no neck.

'You ordered a taxi?'

'Barely a minute ago,' said the traveler, now recognizing the taxi driver Gummi.

'Short way to go. I stick to the peninsula after dark.'

The steam-bath woman had come to the bar, and asked the traveler if she could tag along.

'Tag along or ride along, just as you please,' he heard himself say.

'Thank you,' he then said to Lúter Indriði.

'On the contrary—thank *you*. You're welcome anytime.'

On the contrary—thank *you*. What equivalent would Lúter Indriði have used at Le Meurice—for the world's stars and moneymen?

He was startled from his thoughts when the taxi driver Gummi pushed the bouquet at him: 'Quit forgetting your flowers,' he said gruffly. 'I've got other things to do besides tracking down people like you.'

Because of those damned roses, the traveler had to use all his strength to hold onto the door of the taxi, one-handed. The wind jerked at the door as he sat down, and he just managed to prevent it from blowing off. At the same time, Gummi struggled to get the woman safe and sound to the front seat.

'We get such strong gusts out here on the peninsula,' said the steam-bath woman. She had what the traveler thought was a Skaftafell-region accent.

'Are you from Skaftafell?'

'Half of me is from Western Skaftafell County,' said the steam-bath woman. 'Best place in Iceland. In the countryside.'

'Makes me sad to hear it,' said the traveler. 'I've never been there.' (Why lie about it? Ástamama was from there, and he'd often made trips to the east.)

When Gummi finally drove off, hail was pouring down so thickly that the streetlights dimmed, as well as whatever lights were still lit on the peninsula. They cruised slowly through the withering wall of hail. Inside the taxi, it was silent. Maybe the two shots of whiskey had put the woman to sleep—and it was well past her bedtime. Maybe the traveler himself had nodded off. In any case, he startled when she asked: 'You wouldn't want to come in for a nightcap?'

Wasn't a nightcap the natural follow-up to having begun to get drunk at the Yellow Sheep? No, what nonsense was this? He had to get home to his penthouse and look out over the gas station and reminisce about the greatest bliss in the world, until he passed out in a white chair by the window.

But he wasn't sure whether he dared to go as far as even one block with a taxi driver who was an insuppressible revenant. Wasn't he just going to rob the well-dressed passenger? Hadn't he figured out that here was a man carrying wads of cash?

Maybe he'd accidentally flashed the stack of bills when he was paying at Silfurströnd.

'I can also drive you downtown,' said the taxi driver.

What kind of comment was that? Was that news—that a taxi driver could drive you somewhere? Maybe he was crazy. Dangerous? The steam-bath woman was probably insane too, but hardly dangerous. And he would have an excellent chance with her in a struggle—which wasn't as certain with the taxi driver.

'Maybe I'll take you up on that nightcap,' he said.

'That's more like it,' said the woman, before adding: 'And while I remember it—my name is Sigríður.'

Karl Ástuson, a traveler who wasn't about to say his name, took the banished roses with him, rather than risk having the taxi driver Gummi follow him around with them. He let the woman pay for the taxi—he had no intention of exposing his wallet any more than he already had. He stepped out of the car ahead of her at Silfurströnd 5. In the house next door slept a woman in dark-blue silk pajamas, a woman named Una, who probably dreamed sometimes, not only at night, about their time together. From the New Year's bonfire and all winter long, and then into spring, their final exams at school, and well into summer.

The hailstorm stopped as abruptly as a tap being shut off. The wind held its breath, and a crescent moon lit up a retreating cloud. The cold light fell on the house of the beloved woman, and particularly on a snow-white pine tree at the edge of the garden of number five. Now he was going to go into that house for a nightcap.

A nightcap! Not a complicated thing! But what about the rest of it? How was he supposed to get out of that house? Order a taxi? Wouldn't Taxi Driver Gummi just show up one more time? To finish what he started? What had he started? No, he

37

would have no choice but to sleep in a ghost-house and wait for the buses to start crawling about in the ice-cold dawn of the day. To walk downtown without a hat was impossible. One whipping hailstorm followed another.

If he ever made it back to Iceland, a rental car was an absolute must. He would never again take a chance on ending up in Gummi's cab, with the yellow roses. But he would probably never return. This would be his final trip. He had seen the woman appear at the window. He had seen her lower the blinds. And her shadow had switched off a lamp in the living room. He had been granted this final vision. Now he no longer had any reason to visit Iceland.

Night at Silfurströnd 5

The house of the woman named Sigríður was like her clothes. Well-made, but bland. There were no clean colors in it. The sofas, carpets, and drapes were musky. The paintings were boredom personified. Wait, though—was that a speckled cow peeking through from behind the fog in one painting? The red, iridescent goldfish swimming lazily in a salad bowl on the living-room table didn't belong on this set.

'Why do you have only one goldfish?'

'Too much work taking care of two.'

'Don't you think the poor thing is bored?'

'Hard to say. Icelandic scientists have refuted the theory that goldfish have no short-term memory.'

'In other words, it could remember if it was bored or not.'

'That's precisely the question.'

The guest sat down on a sofa in the corner. The fabric was too fuzzy. It could stick to his clothing. He was very tired and very sleepy and he felt the effects of the two drinks he'd had abnormally much. At best, he would nod off on that woolen sofa until morning and then somehow sneak out without the woman of the house being aware of it. Walk to the nearest bus stop and take a bus downtown. At best, he would have another opportunity to catch a glimpse of Una. His very last glimpse.

'What can I bring you for a nightcap, Karl?'

The woman had started to talk like a bartender at Le Meurice in Paris. And her guest realized what that bartender would say in the French equivalent of 'On the contrary—thank *you*,' as Cousin Lúter had done.

He would say: '*C'est moi.*'

'What do you think?'

'How does red wine sound?'

'Just brilliant, thanks.'

Sigríður at Silfurströnd 5 had taken off her felt coat. She was wearing a grayish-green sweater and her trousers where greenish-gray. Her slippers were earth-brown and spongy-looking. She turned around, and her backside was just as nebulous as her front. She was about 1.68 meters tall, neither chubby nor slim. Nothing on her was too big or too small, but apart from that there was no way to judge her figure, because her clothing hid it completely. Yet one thing was certain: she was well proportioned and had a thin neck. And her movements where elegant. Remarkable, considering she suffered debilitating neuritis.

The woman went to the kitchen and quietly busied herself there. Her guest sat on the sofa and looked at his hands. Lovers of his had remarked that they were beautiful hands. One said: 'Hands like a painter's'—but didn't painters have all kinds of hands? Just like piano players. Some with such short fingers that they could hardly play Rachmaninoff. Or Chopin. No, the woman who talked about painters' fingers had just wanted to say something nice to him, even if it wasn't consistent with the laws of logic.

If he remembered correctly, this woman had been somewhat enamored of him. Married, luckily. Naturally, he tried to snag married women, telling them that he himself was a family man and had a small child. Specifically, a daughter, if pressed. It was a real accomplishment for him (that's how he saw it, anyway) that following most of his affairs, he was spared any theatrics from his lovers.

He'd only found himself in an uncomfortable spot once. It was actually a lover whom he didn't really like very much. She spoke too loudly, with a raspy smoker's voice that he didn't appreciate. She drank too much. Behaved outrageously in bed. Took too much control once they were there. For example, she expressed her wishes directly, and quite brazenly, when she could easily have let him know in a more subtle way. He'd simply made a mistake in his choice of lover. Or rather, he'd seen right away that she wasn't up to snuff, but he took the chance anyway.

This lover went so far as to switch the lights on afterward, sit up in bed and smoke. Without asking if she could smoke. If she'd done so, he would have loaned her an ankle-length robe and slippers and sent her out onto the balcony. And then she'd used his yellow China bowl as an ashtray, a Ming treasure that he used for bonbons while reading in bed. (A tradition he'd maintained since he was little, when Ástamama would bring him bonbons in a bowl at Christmas.)

It would be disgusting to use the Ming bowl again for bonbons. Best to throw it out. Every time he saw it, he would be ruthlessly reminded of the one woman who had no decorum in bed. She was so bent on him achieving orgasm as well that it seemed as if she would never stop until she had reached that goal. She tried trick after trick—and when all else failed, she resorted entirely to hand movements. He had had to tell her TWICE that it probably wasn't going to work for him that time. The first time, she replied coldly: 'Nonsense!' The second time, she said: 'Of course it won't work if you don't want it to.' He was then forced to say that he was sore, and it was impossible to go on.

After she'd turned on the light and was halfway through her cigarette, she put her glasses on and scrutinized him like a judge at an animal exhibition. Then she asked: 'Why do you want the lights off while you do it?'

'I guess I'm just shy by nature,' he said.

'I wouldn't have guessed you were shy.'

'You can't really tell by appearances if people are shy or not.'

'People are my specialty,' she said. 'I don't think you want the lights off because of shyness.'

He dodged her trap. Didn't ask what she did for a living, with people as her specialty. Social worker? Psychiatrist? He said nothing in the hope that he could keep her from delving into personal matters, but she ignored his obvious hint.

'I think you've mistaken me for another woman.'

'I don't know who that could be,' he said.

'You can't think of anyone?' she asked with a laugh, while peering at him over her glasses. He had to admit it—she had a fun laugh. Mischievous. And the smokiness evaporated from her voice when she laughed.

Then she looked at her watch and said she had to go. He was relieved. Usually it was he who took the initiative when it came to leaving. He had to catch a train, catch a flight, whatever it took not to be stuck with a woman in his bed until morning. Preferably, a lover's visit shouldn't take more than three hours. He was a busy man and needed to use his time well—including his time for sleep. Unthinkable to sleep in the same bed as someone else. The quality of his sleep would suffer from it. It would be worse than no sleep at all. Would be unpleasant. Too intimate.

She got out of bed, put on one of his robes, and took her clothing with her into the bathroom. She didn't ask if she could take a shower or borrow his robe. He was more accustomed to lovers who were politer than this one, and he wasn't happy about her making herself so much at home. One thing was certain—he wouldn't be seeing her again.

He dressed and waited for her in the living room. She was

remarkably quick in the shower, and was in the living room in record time, bright and clean as a newly minted penny.

As soon as she walked in, he stood up, hoping that she would take the hint and leave, but she pretended not to notice and sat down on the sofa. So he sat down in the armchair and said nothing.

'I'm starting to sober up,' she said. 'You wouldn't happen to have one for the road, would you?'

'Certainly. What will you have?'

'Gin and tonic.'

He mixed the drink for her, and poured a glass of water for himself.

'Nicely mixed,' she said.

'Thanks,' he said.

'You're also a particularly good lover.'

'Thanks,' he said.

'As good as the best woman.'

'Oh,' he said.

'I find myself preferring women these days.'

'Is that so?'

'Yes,' she said, with a sigh. 'Every man I've met lately seems to have a knack for reminding me uncomfortably of life as it was, with all of the promises made at the beginning—and you can never get back to that point again. When a woman has reached my age, a new man has a way of transforming life into an anachronism. Unless the feeling that time is all wrong comes from within, I don't know. With a woman, this lost-time logic doesn't factor in.'

'I don't really follow.'

'You can get closer to a woman than a man, which means that you're closer to yourself and external time can't touch you as much; it's farther away. And women are usually much better lovers than men. Much more understanding.'

'Do we want to be understood?'

'I think that we all desire to be understood with the understanding of love.'

Did you understand me? Understanding is the worst. The one line of poetry that had nestled in the back of his mind. From the repertoire of the actor with the bass voice—recited with a resounding undertone when he was on his third Dubonnet.

Karl Ástuson had kept quiet for longer than most normal pauses in conversation, or so it seemed, when this evening's lover took a business card from her purse and handed it to him:

'Call me if you think of anything, no matter what it is.'

'Thank you,' he said, and looked at the business card:

Doreen Ash
psychiatrist, psychoanalyst

He stared at the business card and tried to hide his astonishment. Then he said: 'Lovely names you have, and unusual.'

'I don't know how unusual they are,' said Doreen Ash, looking at the man like a highly-trained therapist, which she was.

'What's your father's first name?' asked Karl.

'Why do you ask?'

'I'm curious.'

'You're actually remarkably uncurious, but his name was Carl.'

'Same name as me,' said Karl, 'though I'm guessing he didn't write it with a *K*, like mine.'

'No, with a *C*.'

'Clever!' said Karl, bursting into laughter.

'How about telling me what's so funny?' said Doreen Ash.

'It's a secret,' said Karl.

'I've no doubt about that.'

'So you're both a psychiatrist and a psychoanalyst,' said Karl Ástuson.

'Yes. But I'm thinking about closing my practice. I hate mental illnesses. When they reach a certain point, people become unbearable. No way to reason with them. They say the same thing over and over. Everything revolves around them. The planets, too. Everyone's an idiot except for them. And Dad and Mom are the worst. It's masochistic to a high degree, putting up with such crap all the time. I'd rather be writing.'

'What about?'

'My doctoral thesis was about the relationship between mothers and sons. And then I wrote a book that was an expansion on the same topic. It even sold.'

'What's it called?'

'*Mothersons*.'

'Would it be too complicated to ask the author for a summary?'

'The excessive love of mothers for their sons is a universal problem. Mothers ruin their sons by spoiling them, over-loving them, paying them too much attention, giving them too much affection. They turn them into megalomaniacs or weaklings, if not both, and beyond that, they turn them into unfit husbands and fathers. Their wives then have no choice but to mother them as their mothers did. This creates a vicious circle that you can't break until the mothers understand that they're compensating for emotional frustrations in their marriages, and in their relationships with men in general, by leaning on their sons. In other words, the world is full of wimps and psycho mamas' boys trying to cover up their condition by playing football and setting the world afire and laying as many woman as they possibly can, eternally dissatisfied because no woman is as good as mommy dearest.'

'You don't say,' said Karl Ástuson. 'What about the theory

that all the recent problems of the Western world have their origin in the offspring of a coldhearted mother and an overbearing father?'

'Why, aren't you slick. In the sciences, it's better to stick to one theory at a time. I'm sticking to the destructive force of excessive love.'

'Why is that?'

'Excessive love causes insidious, unfathomable damage and turns men into what I told you before. Emotional coldness causes obvious damage. I'm not interested in anything that's obvious. What kind of mother did you have?'

Karl Ástuson burst out laughing: 'Is this the third degree?'

'Oh, sorry,' said Doreen Ash. 'I'm drunk. And I'm a curious person. And it's a special pleasure not to have to constantly be careful of what you're saying, like in a therapy session. Sometimes when I talk to sane people I feel like a cow that's let outside in the spring—I practically want to jump for joy. So, what was your mother like?'

Karl Ástuson laughed again and said: 'Mom was great. Good-spirited and fun. Always singing. She had an unusually bright voice and could have become a world-famous coloratura soprano. Róbert Abraham said so as well.'

'Sorry, Róbert Abraham?'

'Oh, sorry, Ottóson. I'm not surprised you don't know who he is. She would also sing to me all sorts of stuff she just made up, besides writing a song that was a great hit. She could have gone far. She had everything it took. Looks as well.'

'And how did she look?' asked Doreen Ash.

'Mom was of average height, rather slim, and had a beautiful figure. She had dark hair and a particularly pretty face. She even had a beautiful nose. A straight nose with a slight curve upward. It's called a saddle-nose in Icelandic.'

Doreen Ash said nothing, and he continued: 'She was good

46

in an intangible way, and she loved the world, loved everything in it, particularly people and animals and trees. She knew how to have friends. She knew how to be joyful. Even that, she knew how to do.'

Doreen still said nothing, and he concluded his description: 'She died when I was eighteen.'

This he had never told to any of his lovers, and he was surprised at himself, astounded, in fact, as he sat there on his sofa, at the very break of day, at least one manic bird wide awake and starting to spread its music around the neighborhood with gusto.

'That's not a good age to lose your mom,' said Doreen Ash.

'No it isn't.'

'That's one of the risks people take when they've children. That they die and leave them alone. It no small thing, the burden that people place on their offspring. For example, all offspring have to go through the horror of dying.'

'I've never thought about that.'

'Think about it.'

'I don't have to.'

'No?'

'I'll never have a child.'

'Why not?'

'I'll never live with a woman.'

'Why not?'

'I have my reasons,' said Karl Ástuson, so brusquely that he even startled the psychiatrist.

'Okay.'

'Do you have children?' he then asked, the man who specialized in dodging personal questions.

'No, thank you. And especially not a son to ruin, thank God.'

'You don't think the sciences would have rescued you from doing so?'

'I can't see that they've helped my colleagues. Why would they have helped me? We can be as scientific as we want. The outcome is always the same: we're blind to ourselves. How many doctors do you think I know that have had a serious illness and not seen another doctor before it was too late? I stopped meddling long ago. If I see that something's clearly out of whack with a friend or an acquaintance, I might mention it once, and never again—unless that person brings it up again himself. But that doesn't happen very often. And God forbid that my friends bring up anything that's wrong with me. They would rather end the conversation if it came anywhere close to my problems.'

'Maybe they don't think there's anything to talk about.'

'Typical politeness. You can see very well that I drink too much. And then there's being bisexual, which has its own special complications. You're always in conflict with yourself; it wears you down and tears up your soul in a very unique, noxious way.'

'I can imagine,' said Karl Ástuson sympathetically.

'No, I don't think you can imagine it,' said Doreen Ash, smiling.

'Would you like some more?' said Karl Ástuson, smiling back at her with his sincere, boyish smile. Not only was his smile beautiful, but his teeth were, too. So white and perfectly shaped that others had actually suspected them of being false.

'No thanks. This one went right to my head. That was a pretty strong mix you made. Exactly how I like them. I'm leaving now. Would you please order me a taxi?'

'Certainly,' he said, and rose to order a taxi.

As soon as he said the address, he almost felt as if he were starting to miss Doreen Ash, a lover who was exactly as he didn't like them—overwhelming, and a rule-breaker. After the taxi had been ordered, she sat right there and kept on talking as if time didn't exist.

Karl Ástuson had fallen asleep in a corner of the sofa, with an embroidered cushion in his arms, when the woman of the house brought drinks on a tray. A carafe of red wine, a carafe of water, two wine glasses and two water glasses. She went back and fetched a tray with four types of cheese, olives, nuts, baguette slices, and yellow Easter napkins. She had also tidied up the dilapidated roses and arranged them neatly in a crystal vase on the living-room table, and lit yellow candles in a silver, three-armed candlestick. All of this she had done so silently that he hadn't stirred.

'It's a feast,' he said.

'Easter comes early this year,' she said.

'Easter?'

'Oh, I thought you meant the napkins and the candles.'

'I meant the feast.'

'You can't offer people a drink without providing them something to nibble on. Anything else would be plain barbarism. Did you have any dinner?'

'I don't know if I'd call it that. I've just come off a long-distance flight. Three, rather than one. But at some point tonight I ate a hot dog.'

'At Skúlagata, that's right. Where Gummi picked you up.'

'He didn't really pick me up. The taxi was ordered.'

She left it at that and poured the wine. He didn't feel like asking her how she knew where Gummi had picked him up in his taxi. He settled for her being either a psychic or a spy, if not both. And if she were a spy, and spying on him, she had the wrong person. Sad. Her pay would be docked for it.

The guest watched the woman of the house: how she smeared cheese on a slice of baguette, for instance. She did things as if she'd been trained. She kept her head lowered, like a geisha. Polished hand movements. It reminded him of Ástamama.

49

'Goat's cheese from the Pyrenees,' she said, after laying the slice on his plate.

'Did you just come from there?'

'No, I don't travel anymore. But I have connections.'

Wouldn't people use just such an expression if they really were spying on their neighbors? 'I have connections' is exactly what they would say.

He was starving, and wolfed down the bread. He didn't feel like being there, even though the woman wasn't exactly boring. This nighttime get-together was just so ridiculous. There was something coarse and slightly indecent about him having crept his way into the house next door to Una's. Like a distasteful joke. A gate-crasher at a wake?

But how was he supposed to break out of this hospitable prison? His glass had been filled again; a new slice of baguette with a new type of goat's cheese was on his plate.

He could of course try to call the Hafnarfjörður Taxi Service. There he should be safe from Gummi. Yet who was truly safe from a telepath? No, he wouldn't be able to get away safely from this house in any other vehicle than an ambulance. Of course he would have no problem faking a convincing ache or pain in some appropriate place. The onset of a heart attack, for example. He tried to make himself less conspicuous and to loosen his tie.

'You're tired,' said the steam-bath woman.

'I feel a bit strange,' he said.

'You're welcome to spend the night here. I have a room for you.'

'Thank you.'

'You could take a steam bath before bed.'

'I'm not sure it would be good for me.'

'Everyone benefits from the steam. Except people with heart problems. And you don't look to be that type.

Didn't look like he had heart problems. The man who had never married, never had anything you could call a girlfriend apart from Una, once upon a time, for less than eight months. The man who systematically denied himself the coziness of having a girlfriend or wife, because once upon a time there was Una, because Una was like no other. Not just truly beloved and best beloved, but his only love. There wouldn't be any more, couldn't be any more.

But why not do what everyone else does who couldn't get the person they wanted: have someone else; a woman who was smart, beautiful, charming. He'd met a hundred and two such women, perhaps even more, women with beautiful voices who laughed softly and didn't talk too much, and just were as they were supposed to be. Perky, but not dramatic. Firm, but not bossy. Women who would make life more livable. More meaningful. All he had to do was pick one out of the crowd. Yet wouldn't boredom lay its dead hand over the relationship, if it lacked the right feeling? The basis.

Heart disease? The man who could love none but the one and only, his rightly-named childhood sweetheart, from the moment she walked into the living room with a snowflake on her cap. (Eleven years old and asked him to keep playing, just when he was about to flee from the piano stool.) A man who had a secret room dedicated to music and preferred to tell no one that music was his life; a man who listened to his mother's song on her birthday and other days as well and hummed along to it. A man who had never come to terms with the fact that she died so soon, or with how she had died. A man who kept a lock of his mother's hair and photographs of her in a box like treasures, along with her obituaries. One by a famous poet. And a battered suitcase with a little girl's sweater in it.

It's hard to say precisely how it happened, but he was now in the spare bedroom's bed. He was wearing pajamas that were too big for him, but made of high-quality cotton, Egyptian, probably, like the bed sheets. The bed was as if ordered by Lotta. And an eiderdown duvet. Karl Ástuson was so fond of Icelandic eiderdown duvets that he, who lived alone, had three of them. Two adult-size and one child-size.

She stood in the doorway and said: 'If you change your mind about the steam bath, it's in the basement.'

'Thank you.'

'Good night, Karl.'

'Good night.'

She shut the door behind her and he was alone in the dark and his name was in fact Karl even though he felt like Left-Alone Kalli, as he was when Ástamama switched off the light before he fell asleep. Occasionally, she didn't have the time to lull him to sleep, but would tuck him in, kiss his cheek, and say one prayer. Then she would turn off the light and say good-night, and he would listen to her footsteps descend the stairs.

He would then start crying out of self-pity, and sob over and over beneath the duvet: 'Ástamama come and lull me. Ástamama come and lull me.' The door would be half-open and he would hear the sewing machine whizzing along like a scooter, like a roller coaster, and he would hear the distant humming of Ástamama's 'Yesses'. A whole string of Yesses: YESYESYESYES-YESYESYESYES-YES as the sewing machine sped along Silkbeach, up Tweedhills and down into Ever-glazevalley. So obedient and good was Kalli that he never followed his mother down, not even once. Didn't even walk around the room, but continued to suffer in his bed, as abysmal as children alone can be. Their misery, though, is forgotten as soon as they grow up, meaning adults can never empathize with children's suffering—they no longer have the strength of mind that it takes to remember how overwhelming their suffering was when they were little.

He was wide-awake and longed to fall asleep, to forget his condition. Hugely wealthy Karl, with his own personal assistant and the owner of houses in two of most sought-after places in the world, a lover to hundreds of women—and now he was helpless, motherless, an orphan, and the void in his soul was so vast that it was almost as if he couldn't feel it, or that he had a soul in general. A condition that no amount of tears could improve.

The cause of his tears was the void, the blank space; Una in the house next door. If life was a masterwork painting of a woman against a landscape, than that person, the centerpiece of the image, had been rubbed off with a cloth dipped in turpentine. What remained was a hint of her original color, but nothing of her form. The woman in the painting wasn't where she was supposed to be, and he himself was no painter. The original painter was a sixteenth century master; no one could paint the woman, no one knew how she should be but he himself, Karl Ástuson, who didn't know how to paint. His life's work, apart from financial speculation, consisted of attempting to place all sorts of lovers in the blank space in the painting, where the original woman had been, the one and only.

Every time he had a lover he treated her as if he had Una in his hands. The lights were switched off. He imagined Una, and treated his lover as if he were creating a work of art. It rarely happened that he failed to satisfy his lover fully. He himself never had an orgasm; that was against the rules.

Almost all of his lovers never made a fuss about this. Doreen Ash, the system-crasher, was, of course, an exception. He had ordered a taxi, but she didn't stir from the sofa and said, out of the blue:

'Excuse me for asking, but why do you deny yourself an orgasm?'

'That's just how it goes.'

'So you're a masochist?'

'Nothing of the sort.'

'Masochism is a very tricky thing. I've even suspected myself of it.'

'You don't strike me as being a masochist.'

Then she laughed and stood up and rushed to the door. She was so quick that he wasn't able to open it for her.

She stopped out the door into the glaring morning sun and said: 'There's a gap in your story.'

'How so?'

'You didn't mention your father.'

'You didn't ask.'

'Okay, I'm asking now.'

'I don't know him.'

'Is he Icelandic?'

'I would think so.'

'You don't know where he's from?'

'No.'

'How so?'

'My paternity is unestablished.'

'Did your mother not know who your father was?'

Karl Ástuson laughed and said that that certainly wasn't the case.

'But she didn't tell you who it was?'

'No.'

'How exciting. A purebred motherson.'

'Material for a book, maybe?' said Karl Ástuson.

'Now there's an idea,' said Doreen Ash.

'Motherson—is that even a real term?' he asked.

'It's a great term, precise and transparent. I invented it myself.'

'Sorry for saying so, but it's hardly an original term. All sons are the sons of mothers.'

'Some less than others. Some are less sons of their fathers, too. As has been proven.'

They laughed, and she rushed out to the sidewalk, so swiftly that he couldn't keep up with her.

'Can I pay for your taxi?' asked Karl. 'It's been waiting so long.'

'You cannot,' she said firmly.

He was amused at how firm she was, and couldn't hold back a smile. She stared at him for a second as if she'd had an epiphany, before saying goodnight in her husky voice—despite the night having obviously passed.

She swooped into the car without him being able to give her a farewell kiss, the door slammed, and he stood there with his hands half outstretched, like a man who has just grabbed at thin air, and watched the car until it disappeared around the corner.

He should, of course, take a shower immediately, as the rules stipulated for when a lover had gone, but instead, he had a gin and tonic and enjoyed feeling it warm him from head to toe. He was immensely relieved at having dodged a bullet. At the same time, he was flabbergasted at not having been on the lookout for half-sisters in the past. In a big city, it was statistically very unlikely that he would fish up a half-sister as a lover, but now he'd crossed paths with a woman with a name. From now on he would be forced to ask personal questions, which he'd been so expert at avoiding: full name and country of origin, and all in the first fifteen minutes of the conversation.

Before he finally took a shower, he pulled the smoky sheets off the bed and opened the balcony door. He was on the verge of changing the sheets himself rather than waiting for Immaculata to come, but he decided not to, being out of practice.

He left the balcony door in the lover's room open a crack and went to his bedroom. He couldn't fall asleep. Normally after

a tryst, he had a prevailing feeling of satisfaction over everything having gone as planned, everything as it was supposed to
have been according to protocol, but this time, he was rattled,
and kept remembering various things that he and Doreen had
discussed. He had gone so far as to describe Ástamama to her
in detail. It was a real puzzle, the influence that this person had
on him. And now, three years later, he felt so despondent that
he felt the need to speak to her again.

Speak to Doreen Ash? The psychoanalytic textbook author
who lumped all of humanity together. Sons were like this and
mothers like that, yet mainly such and such. It was coarse,
black and white, no nuances. Primitive. Some people said
that such generalizations amounted to seeing things clearly,
but this was ultimately an insult to human nature in all its
glory and an insult to the complexity of human thought. He
was insulted personally, as well, and on behalf of his mother.
With her American nostrums, Doreen Ash had attempted to
disparage mothers in general, and Ástamama in particular, to
belittle the fact that Kalli Tyke had lived sweet, bright days. It
was a real achievement to bring happiness to a child, that he
knew now, and also that Ástamama was unique, not just as his
mother; she was unforgettable to those who met her, she was
lively and enthusiastic and possessed a special benevolence of
her own, a benevolence that she had invented herself, and that
he wouldn't have been able to describe if he were asked. All
that he would be able to say was that he missed her with all his
heart and would continue to do so all his life.

He frequently dreamed of Ástamama, and she could also
be near him during his waking hours like a living person; for
example in a snowfall, with big flakes swirling around a light-
pole. If he saw or heard something unusual, he imagined what
clever thing Ástamama would have said about it—she who
always came up with things that never would have crossed

another's mind. She had a special sort of humor that could be a bit embarassing, and incredibly to-the-point. Who but Ástamama would have thought of saying, about the orchestra conductor in the last movement of Mahler's *Ninth Symphony*: 'He conducts like a lumberjack.' (It was how his arms chopped the air—not to mention that he was Finnish, of course.)

Una's sense of humor wasn't unlike Ástamama's, and could always make him laugh. He himself could only make lame attempts at jokes. After his mother and Una disappeared from his life, he was left by himself in a laughter-free world.

Lotta brought laughter back to him; she was incredibly funny and witty, in her American way. At the same time, he was reminded of Una's laughter, which he would lack the rest of his life—deprived man that he was. The term described him precisely—deprived man—even if it technically didn't fit him.

In the main, it was in the finest hotels on the world's most beautiful beaches that he could swim through life without remembering too much of what he lacked; far from what really counted: music with kisses and laughter. The two times that he brought Lotta with him to a beach hotel, it had in fact turned out so well that he felt what might be called happiness, each time in its own way. He in his suite, and she in the next room. Available to chat with him when he was in the mood. To leave him in peace when he wanted to be left in peace. Perfect at work, perfect in general. And filled to the brim with laughter, which was actually more than one could ask for, considering all the rest. It was so nice to watch her, to witness the elegance of her movements, like the most beautiful creature in the zoo. Naturally, he wanted to sleep with her, but he knew that it was out of the question to sleep with his right hand, so he gave up the idea.

The trips with Lotta were little parties, miniature get-togethers, an imitation and shadow of the big banquet that he was missing out on. Although these little parties were fun in and of themselves, he felt bitter afterward, because they inevitably reminded him that life was a sequence of sideshows, instead of one main event.

A main event such as the one he had witnessed in the window of Silverströnd 3: a woman in blue pajamas who let down the blind and transformed into a shadow figure who switched off a lamp. Confirmation that he'd been allotted a seven-month banquet in life. Nothing more. Curtain.

Some, however, got no banquet, not so much as one day. That, however, was no consolation; in fact, no such thing was to be had. Least of all by night in a strange house, where he suddenly found himself for some incomprehensible reason. Fear of himself? Fear of strange figures who wouldn't stop popping up? The taxi driver Gummi.

Sigríður with swimming eyes—was she perhaps a sending, plain and simple, and he a doomed man? Who was to end his life in the house next door to Una's? Wasn't that precisely the way that fate worked? Wheels were set in motion. Couldn't be stopped, kept spinning according to their own mechanisms.

He viewed himself from the outside, as if he were watching a thriller about Karl Ástuson. What would happen next? Would he simply be killed, or beaten to a pulp? Who would do it? How? Above all: Why? For nothing, maybe. Weren't people always being killed for nothing? But what kind of death would that be? Even harder to come to terms with than all other deaths combined.

But since he wasn't dead, since he was alive and kicking and free from physical heart ailments, he could still get out of bed and open his curtains; so he got out of bed and drew open his curtains. Una's garden, which faced the sea, lay before his eyes, illuminated by the full moon and garden lanterns. The shrubs were entirely white, as was the pine tree. The duck pond was frozen. Nothing separated the garden from the sea but a slender footpath and sea rocks, the same rocks they had sat on one sunny evening in July, when they leaned their heads together and talked about an endless future, even with children, and he confided in her that sometime in that future, he wanted to have a girl who would preferably be named Ásta, and Una finally told him that she had fallen for him at the New Year's bonfire because he'd been so sweet and kind to little Ásta, his niece.

Now the nighttime world was tranquil again; not a single snowflake fell, there was barely any wind. Nothing living was out and about, other than the ever-moving sea, which joined the land right at the house of the dearly beloved woman. No season changed it, no storms. The sea was unchangeable. It was good and right to conclude his life in the unchangeability in a house by the sea. Preferably not in this house, though; not right away.

He listened to the sea chant about the one thing that his heart and mind yearned for with all their strength and his body along with them, the woman next door, and the sea began chanting her name expressly: 'U-na, U-na, Un-a-a-Un-a.' The same sea as then; when they went down to the water's edge, sat there for hours when the weather permitted it and refused it, sometimes in a drizzle, as if they were waiting for something from the sea: a yacht that would land at their toes, a mermaid, a revelation, or a submarine.

The sea chanted 'U-na, U-na,' and the night guest listened and chanted along and his fingers itched to call across the sea to a woman whose name was actually Ash, as was printed on the business card she'd handed him following their one night of fun, if fun it should be called, three years ago; a woman whom he'd never contacted again and had never even wanted to. But whom he wanted to call now—because he feared for his life, or what? Wasn't he more foolish than doomed?

Karl Ástuson shuffled his feet as he stood there at the window, like a little child who has to pee. He turned away from the window and back to the window, because he literally had no idea which way to turn. He felt he should definitely turn in a specific direction, and stand or fall by it. Yet there was nothing that forbade him from loitering aimlessly by the window until morning, watching the silent earth and chanting sea come together as one.

Eventually, the guest chose a direction and ventured out into the hallway. In the house, Sigríður breathed loudly in her sleep; she hadn't shut the door to her room. Not unlike a mother who keeps vigil, listening for sounds from her child. Stirs if it so much as purrs, no matter how deeply she's dreaming.

Now that he was in the hallway, he should just head straight down to the basement to have a look at the steam room. It was bigger than he expected. It could probably hold ten people. A large corner jacuzzi, a shower stall with streamlined faucets and an overgrown massage shower head. Just like in a luxury hotel, and just as tidy. Why had he never stayed at a hotel where his room had its own private steam bath? What was the point of taking a steam bath with strangers? With other people at all?

He started filling the whirlpool bathtub. His doom would have to wait, if he were doomed. Now he was going to take a shower, and he hastily removed the oversized pajama top, which was perhaps a dead man's. But he stopped before removing his pajama bottoms; he was far too vulnerable in this basement. Clothesless, phoneless.

He went upstairs to fetch his clothes and shoes. The woman of the house stirred. He waited until she slipped back into sleep before taking any more steps. Then he slunk down to the basement like a thief in the night and hung up his clothes.

He planned out his bath ceremony: 1) shower with thorough scrubbing, 2) whirlpool bath, 3) steam bath, 4) cold shower, 5) steam bath, 6) light final rinse.

He was on the second step of his plan, a melting man in a hot bath, when Doreen Ash sailed into his consciousness at full steam. Of course; it would take a specialist to save him from this Silverströnd trap.

He rose and grabbed a towel big enough for two people, dried his arms and chest, reached for his jacket and took out his phone and her business card. His head swam a bit as he sat back down in the burning-hot water, and the digits on the phone began to blur as he tapped in the number of a psychiatrist and book-author in New York.

He was certain that the blurred numbers would end up being wrong. The husky female voice on the phone didn't sound familiar, but he shrugged this off and said his name.

The silence was so prolonged that he was on the verge of asking: 'Is this perhaps a wrong number?', when the woman on the phone suddenly said, as if from a great distance: 'Just a moment.'

He said 'Yes' and lingered in the unreasonably long silence.

When Doreen Ash returned to the phone, her voice sounded normal. Not a trace unnatural. Did she remember Carl Astason? Yes, she did indeed. Just as if she'd been expecting a call from the man that very night. And no, he wasn't bothering her; she had plenty of time.

The caller at Silfurströnd had begun to thank her for her geniality, when he was interrupted in mid-sentence: 'Are you calling from sea? I hear waves lapping.'

Now it was clear that Doreen Ash was drunk. But she was quite good at hiding it.

'No, I'm actually in a bathtub,' he said.

'Oh, is this supposed to be that kind of phone call?' she said, laughing.

'No, sorry,' he replied awkwardly. 'Things have gone a bit haywire here.'

'Well, that's obvious,' she said. 'What's up?'

'Thank you,' he said. 'I would appreciate it if you could give me some advice. I got the impression that you're good at solutions.'

'We'll just have to see about that,' she said, as the clacking of ice cubes gave away her taking a drink.

'What are you drinking?' he asked.

'Gin and tonic, my fourth this evening. My drinking problem has worsened since last time.'

'If I'm to take you at your word, I'll just say: Please do something about it, sooner rather than later.'

'That's what the woman I'm living with says as well. She gives me what for when I drink too much. I deserve it.'

'Have you been together for long?'

'Two years. I see it now, in historical perspective, that you were the reason why I turned my back on men forever.'

'What? Was I that hopeless?'

'It proved that time had put a chokehold on me. What I was telling you about.'

'You shouldn't judge just by me,' said Karl Ástuson. 'I'm a unique case. I've never had a girlfriend except once, when I was a kid. After that I've never met the same woman more than three times—well, I've met one woman five times now, but that's an absolute exception.'

'Having a good mom is no easy thing,' said Doreen Ash in a slurred voice.

'This is about the girlfriend I once had, and whom I can't imagine being replaced by any other.'

An unrestrained sigh in Karl Ástuson's ear, and then a drink. She asked: 'Where in the world are you?'

'I hardly know. In a stranger's house outside Reykjavik.'

62

'What's wrong?'

'I'm not myself. The woman of the house has gone to sleep; she's always taking steam baths and reminds me of a ghost, and I feel like something's going to happen to me.'

'What did I tell you, wimps and psycho mama's boys!'

'What's the point of insulting me? I'm calling you because I'm in trouble.'

'Okay, okay, so tell me more about this trouble of yours.'

'I feel like there's a kind of conspiracy going on.'

'What gives you that feeling?'

'I arrived in this country tonight. It was a spur-of-the-moment trip, so I have a suitcase full of Hawaiian shirts, and I went to a gas station to have a hot dog. It's a milestone gas station—I went there with my girlfriend sometimes, about seventeen years ago, except now it's open 24/7 and has all sorts of bacon-wrapped hot dogs, which really threw me off. And there was this young man that I didn't like. He had bronze-colored hair, I'd seen him before, he lived across the street, and he was giving me the eye, I thought maybe he was going to rob me, so I had the cashier order me a taxi even though I was staying right across the street, and then I had no choice but to let him take me somewhere, of course, and gave him an address, a specific address.

'Just ... an address ... out of the blue ...'

'A woman lives there.'

'The petrol-station woman, yes.'

'Well then, yes. And I stepped out of the car and saw her appear in the window just before she lowered the blinds. She's put on a bit of weight, but I think it suits her well.'

'Okay, okay. Then what?'

'Oh, I couldn't call a taxi, couldn't remember any phone numbers, so I had to walk, the weather was way too cold to walk downtown, and I ended up in a local pub on the outskirts of Reykjavík, called The Yellow Sheep.'

'A local pub on the outskirts of Reykjavík. The Yellow Sheep. Jesus.'

'Well, almost. His name is Lúter. The bartender.'

'Jesus. Go on.'

'Well, all of sudden this woman was there, with such a washed-out look about her, the steam-bath woman, and sort of overly personal in the way she talked, but sharp as a tack. And that's not all—the taxi driver showed up, the one who drove me, with the roses I'd left in the backseat of his car.'

'What roses?'

'Oh, sorry, I'm mixing things up. I forgot to tell you that I bought roses at the gas station. There were no flowers in the apartment. There should always be roses wherever I stay, and I know that Lotta must have made the request, but the landlord simply didn't bother to fulfill it.'

'How did the taxi driver find you at the bar?'

'Well, that's just it!' said Karl Ástuson, raising his voice. 'That's just it! The steam-bath woman actually said that it couldn't have been hard to figure out where I was, because I wouldn't have gone far on foot, what with no hat.'

'Then what happened?'

'Well, when I'd had enough, which I'd actually had for some time, a taxi was ordered, and guess what? The same taxi driver. I was afraid to go alone with him downtown and accepted the woman's invitation for a nightcap at her place. She lives next door.'

'Next door?'

'Next door to my girlfriend.'

'Can't you just spit out the name of this person?'

'I'd rather not—but her name is Una.'

'And you're in the bathtub. What about the woman of the house?'

'She's asleep. This isn't like that.'

'You don't have to give me any reports about this, that, and the other. What you're up to is none of my concern.'

'I just said that to let you know she's sleeping.'

'I'm not sure I understand the problem.'

'All these coincidences have given me a bad feeling. If they're coincidences. Maybe I'm losing my mind?'

'Do I understand correctly that for some years now, Öna has lived in the house next door to the one you're in now, in the bathtub?'

'Yes, I'm in the bathtub, it's down in the basement, there's a steam bath here, among other things.'

'Why don't you try to talk to the woman?'

'I haven't talked to her all these years. It's the middle of the night in this country. Well, it's eternal night half the year here, when it comes down to it.'

'You could try to get the ghost to help you. They must know each other.'

'Yes. Apparently Una has talked to her about me. That's why she must have followed me to The Yellow Sheep. She saw me outside Una's house.'

'Is she married?'

'Yes.'

'Does she have children?'

'No, she doesn't.'

'What do you want to do?'

'That's what I find so terribly hard to decide. I'm afraid to order a taxi, for fear that the same taxi driver will come again. I could wait until the busses start running. I could also steal a hat and a scarf and walk downtown, after drying my hair— there's a blow dryer here—or I could pretend that I'm sick and call an ambulance. That's probably the safest bet, because the taxi driver could be watching the house and notice it if I were to start walking downtown.'

'Aren't you just a little bit mixed up from suddenly finding yourself in the house next door to Öna's?'

'Her name is Una. You've got to admit that this is totally bizarre, with that taxi driver who keeps coming back to haunt me and chases me around with a bouquet of roses.'

'Has it never crossed your mind to try to get her back? Or do you just want it to be like this? One woman after another, instead of her?'

'It was she who left me.'

'Do you think she misses you?'

'I'm sure she does.'

'There is no "sure." The problem is that we can never really know other people. Never. It's fascinating, in a certain sense, but it isn't practical.'

'Even if I'm totally clueless now, I know how it was.'

'If you think she might possibly come back to you, why don't you go for it?'

'The woman is married. I'm afraid of making a fool of myself.'

'Wouldn't it be worth the risk, if there's so much at stake?'

'There's a lot at stake.'

'What's her husband like?'

'He's demanding, or at least he acts like he is. Quite uninteresting. A money man.'

'Aren't you also a money man?'

'I guess.'

'Did she leave you for him?'

'No. No, no. There were a few years between me and him. That's what my sister Fríða tells me.'

'So you also have a sister.'

'A half-sister.'

'You don't say. Older than you?'

66

'Twelve years older.'

'Do you talk to her much?'

'Not really.'

'Why not?'

'Oh, it's got to do with our mother. She played favorites. I was the apple of her eye. After I was born, Fríða got left out a bit, I'm afraid.'

'What did I tell you—mothers lack self-control when it comes to their sons.'

'Are you still writing about that?'

'I've finished a new book; it'll be out soon. The publisher's convinced it'll be a real bestseller. So is my partner.'

'Super.'

'Yes, it is super. I advise you to read it.'

'Of course I'll read it.'

'I should invite you here and ask you what you think. Although Liina's the jealous type.'

'Liina?'

'Yes, my partner. Liina Minuti.'

'Where's she from, with a name like that?'

'Her father's Italian, and her mother's Finnish. Her name is Liina with two i-s.'

'What does she do?'

'She's a psychologist.'

'A psychologist and a psychiatrist living together.'

'Yes. I know. It's a bit textbook sometimes. She takes care of me, with my high blood pressure and all. I feel I need the support. I get more work done than when I'm by myself. Selfish, of course.'

'You didn't need to be in such a hurry to turn your back on men.'

'There was no reason to wait. I saw how the future would be. Eternal disappointments; might as well avoid them, and not dally around deciding to do so. On the other hand, I can admit that I do find it more fun and more giving to be around men than women—sadly, I'm not even a proper lesbian—but I'm closer to women in bed. I'm not counting you. What with your special talents.'

'It is a question of focus.'

'It all comes down to the same thing. Wait a minute—I'm going to get some more.'

And Karl Ástuson took the opportunity to add more hot water to his bath, which was slowly going cold. When Doreen Ash returned to the phone, she said with a slur: 'And what are you going to do about that person next door or wherever she is?'

'I can't just go and knock on her door in the middle of the night.'

'You could give her a call, maybe.'

'I'm sure her husband's at home.'

'I guess you could hang up if he answered the phone. But I would start by waking up the ghost and getting her advice. You said she was smart, didn't you?'

'Yes, and then some. She's downright clairvoyant. Everyone's into hocus pocus in Iceland. And some people literally believe in elves. It was like that when I was little, too. Horrible.'

'All the more reason to get that woman out of there.'

'Well, a lot of people could be saved from less than that.'

'There's one more thing I'm going to say to you. If you take steps to see Yúna and find out, despite all the odds, that you're the one, then you've got to go all-in. If you hesitate, she'll sense it, and that will scare her off. If you're serious about making this happen, then you'd better be ready to put everything you've got into it. Even having a child with her if she really wants it, which I hope for your sake—and for both of your sakes—that she doesn't. Fire your secretary and hire someone older and uglier.'

'You can't ask me to do that. Not an ugly woman. I can't do that.'

'Are you ready to risk everything for this person?'

'I'm not risking anything.'

'Yes, you are. You can't continue with this "sex all over the place".'

'No? Why would I? I wouldn't have to. That's the last thing I would need.'

'That's what you think.'

'That's not what I think. I know it. But what on earth should I do now?'

'I just told you. Wake up the ghost and see what she says. You can start by figuring out what kind of marriage she's in, and if you think there's any sense in it, you can get the ghost to help you make your presence known. Maybe have her start by calling. And you can call me anytime you feel like tonight, if I can help in any way. You're such a favorite of mine, and such a privileged man, that I've never, ever, allowed anyone to disturb me during the night, except once, when a patient I was particularly fond of was a suicide risk. But he killed himself anyway. As I say, privileged man, call if you need me.'

'Thank you, I may just do that. I feel so puny up against this task.'

'When push comes to shove, we're dwarves.'

'What if the woman of the house says that Una is happily married?'

'You could still try, and see what she herself has to say.'

'If I reach her at all.'

'You'll reach her. You're not leaving Iceland without talking to her. It's now or never.'

'Maybe.'

'No maybe. How many lives do you have?'

'One.'

'Remember that. Now go for it.'

'Thank you.'

'You're welcome. Cheers!'

'Cheers! And goodnight, Dween.'

'Goodnight, Karl.'

His bathwater was cold now. Karl Ástuson had begun to shiver, and he felt bad about mispronouncing Doreen's name when he said goodbye. He got out of the bathtub and laid his phone on the shelf above the sink. Looked at the phone as if he doubted that it was actually a phone, let alone that he'd been speaking to Doreen Ash on it.

One short-term project was clear as day: to take a hot shower. When his toes had begun to warm up, he felt peculiarly light-headed. He wasn't thinking about Una in the house next door, not at the moment. But something was in the offing. It was almost frightening for a man who'd gotten used to the idea of having nothing awaiting him in the future. So he turned his back on the future and thought only of warming himself thoroughly, which brought him some relief.

He looked at his bright red legs and toes, turned off the hot water, and gasped for breath under the cold shower as he slowly counted up to a hundred. Following this self-torture, he felt even more relieved, and warm to the core. As he dried behind his ears and between his toes, exactly as Ástamama had taught him, he thought of nothing but floating high on a rushing cloud over an island with a thousand green hills.

He looked in the mirror, combed his hair, and his intention became clear. To get in touch with Una before he left the country. If not tonight, then later. He changed his mind about the conspiracy. He decided to view his situation as if, unless proven otherwise, he had wandered into a neighbor-woman's house by some higher intervention, and now it was up to him to welcome that intervention with open arms and turn it to his favor, instead of stubbing his toes against it like some high threshold.

He got dressed and went upstairs, stopped in the doorway of the bedroom, and said without hesitation: 'I'm sorry to disturb you, but I need to speak to you.'

'Of course you need to speak to me,' said the woman in the bed, as if she'd been awake.

'Just wait in the living room while I tidy myself.'

'Thanks,' he said.

'Or would you like to start brewing coffee?'

'I'll do that,' he said. 'A lot of coffee.'

Karl was finished brewing the coffee when Sigríður came into the kitchen. She'd tied her hair into a ponytail with a bright white elastic band, put on a nice-looking robe in yet another nebulous color. A ghost personified, her face gray from sleep. She had just brushed her teeth and he was relieved there was an odor about her, even if it was just from the toothpaste.

They brought their coffee mugs into the living room. The night guest put his mug on the coffee table and said, before sitting down: You know what this is about, I suppose.

'Tell me anyway.'

'I'm not a German American, I'm Icelandic. My name is Karl, as you know. I've lived in the States for a long time. I'm not used to lying, but tonight things are different. Una is the woman of my life. I've never married and I don't have children, either. I know that Una doesn't have children. I don't know how she feels about me, but if it's anything close to what I feel about her, then I want to give it a try. Preferably now. Will you help me?'

'That's what I'm here for. But it isn't certain you need much help, with things the way they are.'

'Do you have any idea how Una feels about me?'

'I have some idea, but you'll have to ask her yourself.'

71

'How is her husband?'

'He's constantly in her face.'

'How could I get in touch with her now?'

'You could call her on her cell phone.'

'Won't it wake her husband?'

'They don't share the same bedroom. But it's better that he doesn't wake up. He's got jealousy issues, even when there's no reason for it.'

Karl Ástuson felt a bit as if his terrible sense of doom might still play out tonight. That he was predestined to be killed in the house next door to Una's, and not without reason. Wouldn't he also be putting Una in jeopardy, if her husband woke up?

'Do you know if he's a heavy or light sleeper?'

'He sleeps like a rock. A lot of tough guys do.'

'Should I make the call? Or is it better if she hears your voice first, so she won't be as startled?'

'Maybe,' said the ghost of the house. 'Should I call now?'

'No need to wait,' Karl Ástuson heard himself say, in a strong voice, while doubting his own sanity, or whether he was actually awake and situated somewhere in the world, let alone at Silfurströnd 5, in a house that didn't exist when he sat with Una in the garden at number 3 that sunny evening when the future opened up, so deep and radiant that that moment itself paled in comparison.

He watched Sigríður as she made the phone call, and heard her say something that he didn't grasp. Then she handed him the phone.

'Hello and sorry for bothering you,' he said, before heading straight to the matter at hand, without giving Una chance to say as much as 'Hi': Due to a series of very peculiar coincidences, I happen to be in the house next door to yours, and I feel as if it's now or never, to ask whether you would be willing to talk to me, right now, if you can.'

'Yes,' she whispered, and hung up.

Sigríður looked inquisitively at Karl Ástuson. He said that Una was on her way over.

'Then I'd better warm up some pancakes,' the woman said tiredly.

'Pancakes, there's really no need for that,' he said solemnly, like a pastor in a church service.

In retrospect, he didn't understand why he didn't position himself at the window to watch Una from the house next door come walking in the February night to the steps of the house into which he'd strayed or found his way, depending on how one looked at it. But this sight that he never saw, he saw clearer ever afterward than what he saw in reality, when she came through the door wearing a long purple coat, with messy hair.

She looked at him and smiled, as if she were about to thank him for the time they had previously shared. Then she abruptly bent down and removed her leather boots. She hadn't taken the time to put on socks. He felt a lump in his throat as he looked at her toes and the legs of her pajama trousers. He wanted to ask her if he could take her coat, but didn't dare speak, for fear his voice would quaver. That was not an option as a prelude. This was a so-called fateful moment, and he mustn't blow it by bursting into tears right there in front of the wardrobe.

She removed her own coat. He took it and hung it up, like a queen's butler, and there stood Una in the hallway in dark-blue silk pajamas, clutching a big bottle-green purse as if it were her guardian spirit. This was how attached a woman could be to her purse—making sure to bring it along rather than dressing in haste—even if it were just socks—if she unexpectedly had to pay a visit to a neighboring house in the middle of the night.

'Hi, Una dear, please come in,' said Sigríður. 'Might I loan you a robe and some socks?'

'I would appreciate that.'

73

Una preceded Karl into the living room and sat down on the sofa. He took a seat in an armchair across from her. She seemed distraught and stared into a corner, as if she saw a malevolent spirit that wouldn't disappear even if she looked away.

Karl Ástuson hung his head and examined the rug at a spot farthest from Una's toes. Yet these female toes continued to exert such an influence on him that he didn't risk opening his mouth until they were safely tucked into woolen socks. Only then did he lean forward in his chair and reach with one hand across the table, as if to greet her with a handshake. She took his hand firmly, and there they sat, as if frozen in a prolonged handshake.

'We may not have much time now,' he said, 'but I decided not to leave the country without speaking to you. A psychiatrist friend of mine helped me to see things clearly.'

'Are you seeing a psychiatrist?'

'No,' he said. 'But maybe I should be.'

'I've been in therapy for five years,' said Una. 'I guess I went in the hope that my psychiatrist would help me get out of my marriage, but nothing works. They only help those who help themselves—it's always the same old story.'

'Are you unhappy?' asked Karl, as if he were asking about the weather forecast. And Una replied as if she'd seen it, and had this to report: 'It's a big word, happiness. Same for unhappiness.'

'That's what my mother used to say,' he said.

'I know,' said Una. 'You told me.'

'I'd forgotten I told you that.'

'How could you forget?'

'I don't know. But I've never forgotten you, not for a single day.'

She said nothing.

'I've never been married. Haven't even had a girlfriend.'

74

'I miss you, too. All the time.'

Karl Ástuson loosened his grip rather carelessly, bumping his hand against the coffee mug and splashing himself with coffee. He wiped it off awkwardly with a yellow Easter napkin, then stood up and sat next to Una and gazed at her profile. She lowered her eyes and stared at her hands.

They had changed as much as her face. The years had created tiny wrinkles around her eyes and mouth, and her cheeks were fuller than before. She had a slight double chin, perhaps because she was looking down. She didn't look particularly young for a thirty-seven-year-old, but he found her incredibly beautiful. He envied time for having run its hands over that dear face. At the same time, he cherished every minute of time that had fallen onto that face, and it was his dearest wish to be present for as many of the minutes that were yet to fall on it.

I miss you, too. All the time. That being the case, he felt that it must be safe to put his arms around Una. He did so, and said: 'May I ask you to come with me?'

'Where?'

'I live in two places: on Long Island and in the south of France. Just outside of Arles.'

'When?'

'Now.'

'Now?'

'I trust nothing but the moment. The moment is now.'

'How will we go about it?'

'We can catch a flight if we leave right away. Do you have your passport?'

'It's in my purse, by complete coincidence.'

'I've stopped believing in coincidences.'

'What about Ingi Bói, he'll wake up and I'll just be gone?'

'You can send him a text message before you board the

plane.'

'Can't this wait until tomorrow?'

'I don't trust tomorrow.'

'How so?'

'If we wait, there's a chance that this won't work. I want to take you with me away from this house. Now.'

Karl Ástuson lifted the arm that he had put around Una's shoulders, reached for a pancake and bit off half of it, to emphasize his dedication to his plan. He chewed it calmly, unhurriedly.

'Yes, but I love my house,' said Una.

'You'll have other houses in its stead, better ones. Two rather than one.'

'No house can replace my house,' said Una. 'That house is my life.'

'A house is a house,' said Karl. 'A life is a life.'

'You're serious about this,' said Una.

'This is the only thing I've ever been serious about. Apart from our seven months.'

'Seven months,' said Una. 'That stretched themselves over our lives, all the way to this moment.'

'The August morning when we separated is chasing us down.'

'One day I'll tell you what happened,' she said.

'As you wish,' he said, without being entirely certain whether he wanted to know what happened. He had preferred to imagine that nothing had happened, that she'd just gone her own way like every other nineteen-year-old girl who wasn't ready to spend the rest of her life with someone. He'd always shoved aside thoughts of why his girl had broken up with him.

What apathy was that? What denial was that? And why didn't he ask her a single thing there at the kitchen table when she broke up with him? Was it because he was a wimp, maybe?

When he had thought that heroes and gentlemen did as he did. Immediately get to their feet, elegant and dignified, as a sign that a sweetheart of theirs who wanted to leave could do so freely.

Now Una looked him in the eye, the man who loved her eternally, for the first time since that Tuesday morning seventeen years ago. Judging by her expression, he would have thought that a lover of hers had died in the same room. Then she stood up and slowly straightened her back, in precisely the same way she had since they were young, which Karl knew by heart. She mumbled so softly that he saw, rather than heard her say: I'll ask Sigríður to lend me some clothes.

At that moment, he felt relief, utter relief, perhaps the way one feels when one learns that a disease isn't necessarily lethal. He felt neither hotter nor colder; he just gulped down more coffee and plastered the remainder of his pancake with butter. It wasn't often that he got a chance to have Icelandic butter.

He preferred not to call a taxi to take them to the airport—for fear of Gummi turning up—and he couldn't call an ambulance. He hoped that Sigríður had a car—and that she would offer to drive them, which would be safest by far. Number one was to get out of the house at record speed, before an enraged husband woke up next door. And now he really had a reason to be enraged. It was every man's nightmare that his wife would run off with an old boyfriend, under cover of night. Without the slightest hint in advance. It was too bad it had to be like that, but there was no other way. It was now or never.

And now he was alone in that ghost-plagued living room at a critical moment. The women disappeared like that, without saying a word. Just then, Una would be trying on clothing of no particular color, clothing in which she would be following him across the ocean. What ocean? As soon as that became clear, he would have to call Lotta and have her make preparations for their arrival. He was anxious about what he would say to Lotta: I'm not coming alone. Unforeseen things have happened here. It sounded like an accident. And the news would in fact hit her hard. She had probably stopped hoping, after all these years, that they would ever be together. But what she hoped for, and believed, was that the situation would remain the same, allowing her to continue to gather the crumbs that fell off the table; among them a trip with her *master* once a year or so.

He felt bad about how his new status—no longer single—would hurt Lotta. She would view it as a betrayal. Even if he had never promised her anything, he had made it very clear that he would never tie himself down. On the other hand, he had, even with that precaution, always tried to be extremely careful that she didn't misinterpret him. But since when was love logical? People in love find occasion to hope in every look and every gesture. He must have kindled her hopes by telling her a secret, which he'd never told anyone, over dinner at *The Nightingale*. He'd told her about Ástamama, how she'd prepared him for life without her.

He'd been lucky enough to get a table with the most scenic view at *The Nightingale*, of a forest of skyscrapers and a lake (and was chuffed with himself for still knowing how to reserve a table, after all the years that Lotta had seen to that). Such a dinner was possible at such short notice only because Lotta kept some nice outfits handy at work. It was only twice a year or so that she had to use them, but as ever, Lotta was ready for everything. She came walking out of the office looking radiant in a mint-green silk gown, and he opened a well-chosen champagne bottle.

It had been a long time since he'd been in such a good mood. Business—which he described as speculation—had been going particularly well. In one week he had raked in larger sums than ever before in such a short period. What he was going to do with all that money, however, was a slight cause for concern. He would have to work hard to find the best ways to multiply it. Acceptable risk; putting few eggs into many baskets—that was the key.

Of course he was tipsy from the champagne and other drinks on top of it—otherwise he would never have started talking about Ástamama. Not like that. He hadn't told anyone about her dying moments, about when she was dead. No one but Una, and then only in limited fashion. Naturally, he couldn't describe it in detail, and that he hadn't done; particularly leaving out how he himself had wanted to die. How he had taken ill, but hadn't managed to die.

Perhaps what saved him was not being able to do that to Ástamama, to leave just yet, because of course she would have wanted her favorite to continue to exist on her favorite planet, with all that was in it, mountains and lakes and birds and trees—and people.

He told Lotta how calm and collected his mother had been throughout her illness, how focused she had been in preparing him, how beautifully she had spoken to him. Soon after the diagnosis, before the illness began to put its real mark on her, she spent a whole evening telling her son how much he meant to her, how indescribably happy she had been when he was born, that he meant everything to her, that he was the most wonderful person she knew. That she hadn't created him—he had created himself; that he was miraculous. (This was the word she had used for Karl Ástuson: 'miraculous.' A somewhat Biblical expression, he realized when he grew older, but he still loved it.)

Then the preparations took over. Day after day, week after week, she prepared Karl Ástuson for the inevitable. That she was saying goodbye to the world and everything in it, including, and especially, her son. He was certain that he wouldn't have survived losing her without her first having prepared him, because before she left, she taught him how to exist without her.

She urged him, above all, to choose his wife well. The best thing there is, is to be happily married; the second-best is to be alone. She impressed upon him that a spouse had to be interesting and genial; someone you could talk to about everything under the sun. What was most important in a wife was a good character.

'You mustn't make the mistake of marrying a temperamental bitch, Kalli dear. It's so unpleasant being around demanding, cranky people. In my opinion, such people can shorten your life, not to mention the quality of it. And character defects can't be put right in one fell swoop. Not at all, usually.'

'The problem,' Ástamama added, 'is that we're not good judges of character when we're young. I would never have dreamed of taking up with Toddi, Fríða's father, if I'd been a few years older and wiser. Try to get your head and your heart to work together. As soon as you notice that your girlfriend has some character defects that won't be easy to live with, if she does, then get out of there as quickly as you can, before you're stuck. Choosing the wrong spouse can ruin your whole life.

'Be particularly cautious about letting a woman grab you by the throat. Women can be mean without men realizing it. Men can be incredibly naïve. Which can be lovely, but detrimental to them.'

And Karl Ástuson told Lotta about how, by means of all sorts of practical advice, for example recipes for fish chowder and Swiss rolls and how to choose the right woman, his mother had, for quite some time, managed to direct attention away from her own situation. They had talked for hours about everything but her illness; mainly about his future. What he wanted, how he wanted to continue his education, what sort of house he wanted to live in. She wanted to see into the future, visualize the time when she would no longer be there—she wanted to see her Kalli after five years, after ten years, after twenty years.

'How many children do you want to have?' she asked.

'One girl. I want to name her Ásta.'

'Give her my regards,' said Ástamama. She could say such things without being sentimental, without calling forth tears. She could say them directly—that she who was dying gave her regards to a grandchild who was far from existing.

One incredible thing was the rules she had about how long Kalli was allowed to spend with her once she'd entered the worst stage of her illness.

'If you want to keep me forever in your memory, Kalli dear,' she said, 'then this is the most important thing. Not to be loitering by my side at all hours when it's nearing the end. Young people shouldn't be burdened with such things. We're not fully grown and fully hardened until around thirty, at least—and you're eleven years short of that.' Then she smiled and kissed him, and showed him out the door.

'What an incredible woman,' said Lotta.

'She was. Simply incredible. If I may say so myself.'

Lotta shed tears onto the bosom of her mint-green gown in memory of a woman she'd never known, and Karl Ástuson would have joined her in her teary tribute if he hadn't given up crying by that point.

'Let's leave it at that,' he said. 'The wine has loosened my tongue.'

'It's so indescribably sad,' said Lotta. 'But beautiful at the same time.'

'Beautiful too, yes. We mustn't forget that,' he repeated, like a personified echo, and they dove into the dessert, vanilla-scented panna cotta, a world-class delicacy. It had won first prize at an international competition for desserts in Rio de Janeiro the year before.

As they ate their prize-winning dessert, Karl Ástuson tried to regain his composure. He became more formal and serene, wanting to ensure that Lotta didn't misunderstand this unexpected confession of his deepest emotions. That he didn't continue to mislead her, if that's what he had been doing.

He had never before spoken to her in such a personal manner, the woman with whom he had worked closely for five years—and he couldn't allow himself to do so again. It would give her false hopes. It was wrong to treat people like that.

After asking for the bill, he suggested that they take separate taxis, so that he could get home as soon as possible; there was a small matter that needed his attention.

'As you wish, Master,' said Lotta, in her most disciplined voice—although a slight twitch around her mouth betrayed her disappointment. This dinner and their conversation about Ástamama didn't herald the big change, the long-awaited milestone; she was on her way home, alone.

He snapped out of his thoughts about Lotta. What was going on? The most important event of his life was at hand and Lotta was in his way—she who normally assisted him and was at his side, like an extension of his arm. He had work to do. He had to get himself and Una out of the country. First make a necessary stop at the penthouse apartment, with its view over a gas station. His laptop was there, and he simply couldn't leave it behind. The stack of Hawaiian shirts, and the black pajamas, he would gladly have left, and had Lotta call and make arrangements to donate them to the Red Cross.

He had no idea how long they'd been trying on clothes; whether Una and Sigríður had been gone for five minutes or ten minutes, or even fifteen. He was becoming anxious.

Una hadn't said anything about going with him. Instead, she

had said: 'Can you lend me some clothes?' Could they possibly be tricking him? Had they gone out through the basement door and over to Una's house, thinking that he was crazy, and now sought refuge with that idiot Ingi Bói?

He didn't hear a sound from them—was that normal? He stood up and walked toward the bedroom. His heart beat faster when he heard the women's voices. Sigríður stuck her head out the doorway and asked: 'Missing us already?'

'No, no,' he said awkwardly. 'There's just so much at stake that I'm feeling a bit antsy.'

'We're almost done,' said Sigríður. 'It isn't so easy finding clothes of mine to fit Una.'

He sat back down on the sofa, spread a pancake with mature goat's cheese and ate it as if in a rush, then gulped down a mug of coffee, while thinking that now he'd have to go to the bathroom again and again after all this coffee, which wasn't exactly practical during an escape. No, this wasn't an escape; it was a kidnapping. He was kidnapping a woman. Hardly good manners. But there isn't always room for good manners in fairytales.

He pictured Una in her long purple coat, walking down the sidewalk to Sigríður's house. The scene reminded him of a prisoner exchange in a movie. But the man who was supposed to be looking after Una in her old place was sleeping, and the one who was supposed to welcome her hadn't had the sense to watch her through the window, to make sure that everything went as it should.

Karl Ástuson laughed when Una came into the living room.

'I was careful not to look in the mirror,' she said.

'Best to leave it at that,' he said.

'Those are the thanks I get?' said Sigríður in her most piteous tone, and they all laughed.

A glamorous woman under forty had been transformed into

a dowdy woman of sixty, wearing woolen trousers that were far too short and a russet sweater that was far too big. There was no way she could put her coat on over that bulky thing.

'I'll have to wear my pajama top,' she said. 'Doesn't matter—it could be a blouse.'

It was his destiny to make a journey with a woman in a dark-blue pajama top, an unreal garment that he'd seen through a window, and had prepared himself to dream about for the rest of his life. Instead, he was being granted the chance to touch it as much as he pleased. He might as well do so right away, he thought—and he stroked the sleeve up to the shoulder and said: 'What a beautiful color this is.'

'Afternoon-blue,' said Una.

'Beautiful! Did you come up with that yourself?'

'I don't know. I thought of my life as if it were afternoon-blue.'

'At my house down south, there's endless sunshine. Would you like to go there?'

'Can I think about it on the way to the airport? I'm not sure. Does it not matter to you whether we go south or west?'

'I was going to go west, but I can go south first, if you prefer.'

'It's not too much trouble for you?'

'No.'

He embraced Una quickly, firmly, and whispered in her ear: 'Now you're coming with me.'

'I'm coming with you,' she answered.

He held Una's hand going down the front steps and she leaned into him as if she felt dizzy. He was in fact fearful of Ingi Bói. He truly expected him to come storming out of the house with a gun—having woken to the slamming of a car door, a car being started in the middle of night—and his wife gone from her bed.

Sigríður sat in the back seat and let Karl do the driving. Now Una was suddenly in the front seat with him, and he felt

84

slightly shy about driving her. He tilted his head and looked at her leather boots. They weren't all that unconvincing with those short woolen trousers, luckily. He would have been terribly embarrassed about Una being dressed like a clown on their first journey together.

Later, she told him that she'd been close to tears leaving her house, because she loved that house as much as one can love a house, or more, actually. She loved it as an individual and left it as a dear friend whom she would never speak to again.

They said nothing on the empty streets in the darkness alongside the sea. The driver shortened this silence, which he was part of, by stepping on the pedal, far surpassing the speed limit, even running one red light.

When they came to where Karl was supposed to have been staying, Sigríður waited in the car, but Una wanted to see the apartment. She walked in ahead of him, went straight to the living-room window and pulled back the curtains. He rushed over to her as if she were at risk of vanishing into thin air before the view of a gas station and the restless sea.

'It's a coincidence,' he said. 'Another one. My secretary arranges my accommodations. But I had a hot dog there tonight. With everything but raw onions. That wasn't a coincidence.'

Una smiled her wonderful smile. It was smile number two in the new era, which had begun with the first in Sigríður's hallway—the smile that had opened up the sky, unwound the banks of clouds and dissolved the thick fog.

He stared enchanted at the long smile that lingered on her face despite it being formally gone, and then asked: 'Do you come to this gas station sometimes?'

'I'm not telling,' she said with her mischievous smile, which was so fleeting that it was hardly visible until afterward.

He began folding his clothes and packing them. He

85

hurriedly stuck his black pajamas into his laptop bag so she wouldn't touch them. Black pajamas. Wasn't there something seductive about black pajamas? Might his lovers have thought of him as a philanderer? The idea had never crossed his mind before. Might Una think of him as a philanderer if she knew about all his lovers?

He looked at the closed laptop bag holding the black pajamas, and decided never to tell Una about his lovers; only that he had had one or two. At that same time he realized, just now, finally, that Lotta had been a substitute girlfriend, that she had made his solitude easy; she had taken care of him as a real girlfriend would have done. She would have ironed his shirts happily if he had not forbidden her from doing so and been steadfast about taking them to the drycleaners himself.

Una had returned to the window, and he went to her and put his arm around her. She laid her head on his shoulder and they stood side-by-side looking down at the gas station, as they had done from a different perspective one evening a long time ago, and then more nights afterward.

'I can't believe this,' she said.

'Yet you will see that it's true,' said he.

He wanted to kiss her, but wasn't sure this was the right moment. So he didn't, and instead took her hand in both of his.

'I remember,' she said.

And it was true—if her hands were cold, back then, he would warm them, long and carefully, as if they were made from eggshell-thin china.

They held hands as they left the apartment and got into the elevator, stood close together down six floors, as if their upper arms had grown into one, Karl leaning to one side from the weight of the bags in his free hand. They found Sigríður sleeping in the car. And Una began to nod as soon as they turned onto the Breiðholt highway, looking not a whit as if she were being abducted.

Karl couldn't take his eyes off the road, which was icy in spots. One time, at a traffic light, he looked at Una and she smiled her wonderful smile and laid her hand ever so lightly on his. Then she continued dozing off and waking, the main character on a nerve-wracking journey.

'Would you rather go south or west?' asked Karl, as they passed the turnoff to Grindavík.

'Shouldn't we start in the south?' she replied. 'The flights to the west don't leave until later today.'

'That's right—but we could leave now on a connecting flight to London, for instance, if we want to go west.'

'South to good weather—how does that sound?' she said.

'South to Paradise,' he said. 'The almond trees and cherry trees are in bloom now.'

'It's just like dream,' she said.

'Then we'll fly to the dream. To Marseille, with a layover in Paris, he said.

'Are you sure there's a flight to Paris today?' she asked.

'We're still heading south,' said he, 'even if it's through another city.'

'And the money's no problem?'

'No problem,' said he.

Una burst into tears when she said goodbye to Sigríður. Karl had no idea what to say to her: 'I can never thank you enough,' was what he ended up saying, before kissing her on the cheek, which was pasty, like her personality. He had to refrain from wiping his mouth while she was still in eyesight.

From that pasty kiss when he said goodbye to Sigríður, until Paris, Karl Ástuson was in a state of consciousness that he had never experienced before. As if he were half-asleep, yet still had the sense to do everything right, down to the smallest details.

87

Have Una wait at the proper distance while he bought the tickets (not a crucial detail, but it was better to be cautious, in case the person at the ticket desk recognized her). He also had her wait while he bought clothes for her at the duty free shop. It would have drawn too much attention, someone walking in in a pajama top and trying on clothes. And he put his expertise to good use, finding Una a bright skirt and red sweater in record time. Size forty-two, one size larger than last time.

While Una was in the bathroom changing, Karl was so focused, despite his somnambulist state, that he bought a bottle of cod-liver oil. As if that weren't enough, he also had the presence of mind to call Lotta. Without telling her about the woman he had in tow. Just that he was on his way south. Let her know to have the house ready; he would be there around four local time. Reserve a table at The Golden Swallow for nine. For one, yes.

When Una returned from her little expedition, impeccably dressed, Karl confided in her that cod-liver oil was the only thing from Iceland that he couldn't live without, apart from her. As was now proven. In return he received a mischievous smile, and it was then that he started to believe this journey with Una was for real—stopped being afraid that she would back out; in the jet bridge, for that matter. It was then that he knew for certain that she was going with him all the way, not just to Paris, but all the way south, where he had a two-hundred year old house, in a place blessed with sunshine three hundred days a year.

When they arrived at their gate, with only half an hour until departure, they put together a text message for Ingi Bói. *Made a snap decision about taking a holiday. More soon. Don't worry. U.*

After sending the message, she looked up and said: 'Poor him.'

'Poor *you*,' said Karl. 'You deserve better than to have a bully for a husband.'

Una looked at him as if she'd had an epiphany. Had this obvious fact never dawned on her? That she deserved better than to have a husband who dominated her? No, obvious facts were often the last to dawn on people. He knew it only too well.

Karl could not imagine how Una viewed him after they'd settled into their seats on the airplane, but this much was certain: she didn't look like a woman who was about to start a new life out of the blue, a chosen person, with happiness coming her way. Here was a sleepy woman who had forgotten to comb her hair, sitting next to a random acquaintance on a flight to Paris.

Karl wanted to ask her how she was feeling, but decided not to. He mustn't disturb her. He was just supposed to be there and see to their journey, like a tour guide; be alert to the passenger's needs and try to make the trip as smooth as possible. Because it isn't easy being abducted, even though the abductee doesn't need to think about anything.

'You look so elegant in your new clothes,' he said.

'Well-chosen on your part,' she said. 'And they fit perfectly.'

'This is just the beginning,' he said. 'Now the son of the seamstress will start building up your wardrobe.'

'It will take a lot of thought, starting completely from scratch.'

'The son of the seamstress won't quail at the task.'

'You were probably the only boy in high school who knew anything about fabrics.'

'Well, I was swaddled in tulle and cut my teeth on muslin. So it's literally in my blood. With pins.'

'The son of the seamstress must have taken it personally, seeing his beloved in Sigríður's woolens.'

'I should have taken a photo.'

The stewardess brought blankets and pillows. Karl helped Una spread the blanket over herself and they tried to settle in for sleep, with all the twisting and turning it takes to find the right position in an airplane seat.

He didn't take his eyes off her face as her worried look faded and gave way to a little smile. Then she was asleep—and a new wave of panic and doubt hit Karl Ástuson. What was he doing?

He was stealing away his love—another man's wife and no child's mother. That wasn't the problem; it was going like clockwork, as if the operation had been planned in detail by a professional.

But the problem was what came next—no less than the life ahead of them, in its entirety. What guarantee did he have, for instance, that Una would get along with him, a new man in a new era? He didn't think he'd changed that much since high school, but since when could you count on what you thought about yourself? In the past or future?

That he wouldn't get along with Una was out of the question. Una was as she had always been. He knew where he stood with her. She was crystal clear, yet not tiresomely transparent and predictable, whatever she did.

Herein lay his doubt: was he man enough to handle the heroic task of picking up where he'd left off with this woman? And his worst doubt had become visible on the surface and was growing with frightening speed—an iceberg in the middle of a sailing route; how would it be to sleep with his childhood sweetheart on the other side of the sea, now that that moment was in sight?

'Your hands are cold,' said Una, when she stirred and laid her hand on his.

It was true. This talented lover shivered at the dreadful thought that he might not be able to satisfy her. That he would quite simply be unable to perform; that he would screw up their lovemaking so badly, in every way. That she would turn away from him and, in the worst case scenario, take the next flight back to Iceland.

As Una continued to slumber on his shoulder, and he held her tightly and drew strength from the embrace, he pulled himself together and came up with a three-phase plan. He would:

First: not make any neurotic decisions. Not seize the moment until Una was definitely ready.

Second: take it incredibly slowly, bridging a time-span of seventeen years at a snail's pace.

Third: imagine that she was a lover whom he would treat as if she were Una. To prevent overwhelming emotions from getting in the way of things.

He accepted the champagne and newspaper offered and began flipping through the pages of the *Morgunblaðið* daily as if it were from Mars. Was it there that he'd been, out in space, on Silfurströnd by the Milky Way, when a woman by the name of Una came sailing on a starship to him? It had taken her seventeen years to reach him; a long voyage on the scale of a human lifetime—but just a blink in the eye of eternity.

He read three obituaries in succession as he finished his champagne. People living and dead were called by nicknames that sounded like jokes. For example, there were twins named Robbi and Bobbi. One piece read as if it were making fun of the deceased, a man who had died in the prime of life. The article said that he had passed away in the prime of his life. Was this a typo, or a silly allusion to the fact that the man had been a respected linguist?

Karl Ástuson was so absorbed in the way that Icelanders wrote about death that he didn't notice the plane taking off, and wasn't aware of it until the lights on the ground had become tiny dots; that a new day was dawning in a new dimension, in the sky below, above, and to the sides.

In that dimension, time was made of flexible material. The fact that Una was sailing beside him through the air meant nothing other than that they had bent time into a circle, linking the decades. From now on, the two of them would be side by side, for as long as time allowed in new countries; the kind of time to which we must all bow down in the end, the kind of time that we do not bend—but where we exist as a memory, as long as someone living remembers us.

The fog of worry that had surrounded him so densely his last hours in Iceland, forcing him to proceed as carefully as if to avoid bumping into walls, now dissipated after his reading of three obituaries, and Karl Ástuson dozed off and slept like a log until the airplane touched French soil.

Yes-tango

One peculiar thing was that as long as Karl and Una lived, they spoke very little of their week in the little castle Beauséjour, south of the city of Arles and north of the Camargue, which is called an alluvial plain, but is actually a triangular island with high reeds and ponds and its own unique animal life between the two arms of the Rhone River delta and the Mediterranean Sea. ('The place in the world where heaven replaces earth,' said Una.)

Karl Ástuson came up with a word for that week, calling it 'Dreamtime'—a word that he never said out loud, but kept to himself like a secret key, a word that made life worth living, a word that one could have on one's lips when life was at its end.

They never parted from one another, at their new start, these lovers of past and new times. When they went for walks in the Camargue, where the horizon is an expanse of giant reeds and a long water-mirror, with clouds and exotic pink birds (flamingos, which Una said looked like candy on stilts), they stuck as close together as possible without tripping each other up. The only way to do this is for the man to hold the woman tightly around her shoulders as she holds the small of his back. A method that's both delightful and tiring at once. When they had their morning coffee in the conservatory, they sat together and held hands for as long as their breakfast allowed. Karl became adept at drinking his coffee with his left hand.

Most of the time, their demeanors were serious, these people who loved to laugh; almost as if they were facing a great trial of strength and will. Yet they lived in wonder and joy at their shared experiences, whether big or small: memories of kisses or new kisses, the apricot jam from Henriette, *vin de sable* from the region, which they called 'sand-rosé,' or their drives through a landscape that had become part of the global consciousness through world-famous images. Now adorned with blossoming, cloud-like treetops—exuberance that bordered on mirage—particularly for an Icelander, no matter how well-traveled he might be.

Una fit into this environment like a local from a neighboring district—she who'd never even been to France. Her road had always led to Italy. At the market she knew all the vegetable varieties and made her selections no less critically than the French themselves. (She asked about wild asparagus, but unfortunately, it wasn't quite in season.) And to top it off, she spoke French, the darling, however she had managed that, and Karl stared at her as if she were speaking in tongues.

In the house and the garden at Beauséjour, she seemed so at home that she may as well have been the housemistress there, alongside Karl, the entire nine years that he'd owned the place. During that time, he had done what he could to coordinate everything in Una-style. By choosing her colors, for instance, which weren't necessarily his colors. And whether it was because of this or something else, she said, as soon as she stepped through the door: 'I feel like I've been here before.' And Karl answered: 'You have been.'

Of course it hadn't escaped him that he was buying for Una when he went to vintage stores, when he ordered the white leather sofa from Italy, an unlikely piece of furniture that happened to really work in its new home, accentuating the

Mediterranean exuberance in the stone floor tiles and making the floor seem to dance.

He had selected and decorated everything in Beauséjour in her spirit, without having believed for one minute that she would return to him, without imagining that she could ever become his wife, in the future, in the unlikely case that the present would condescend to zigzag its way there.

Still, there had been moments when he sat in the double swing, particularly one autumn, late, when he imagined Una in the garden, Una picking the olives, green and purple, and she appeared to him as if in the flesh.

'Una,' he had said aloud, 'I know how to cure olives.'

He didn't tell her that she'd been there with him, that he'd addressed her there by the tree, but he repeated what he'd said then, that he knew how to cure olives, and added that they should return in the autumn when they were ripe.

They said little or nothing about what once was, but shed some tears over lost time. Karl Ástuson hadn't wept since he sat on a step in Grand Central Station his first day in New York. Now he wept again and buried his face in Una's hair; it happened more than once, and he wasn't ashamed.

After they made love for the first time, he wept. He'd noticed a puzzled expression on Una's face, a look that he didn't recognize and that drove him to tears for the first time in his life—but certainly not the last. Regret over the years he had missed out on, and she as well. Joy that the major task had been accomplished: building a bridge from his former life through the void, over to life itself. But most of all, he wept with relief at how they had melted together into one person as they were making love. It was impossible to come closer to another person, soul and all, and there he had longed to go, all the way to Una. He had never wanted anything else.

Their first night in Beauséjour, after dinner at The Golden

Swallow, Karl Ástuson sat down at the grand piano and played a waltz by Chopin, though not *Valse de l'adieu*, as he had played in the living room of old, and, as expected, Una listened entranced on the white sofa. He played just this one piece, and then sat down quite close beside her on the sofa. It was she who slowly leaned over to him and put her arm around his neck, and it was he who began to kiss her, at first softly, and then firmly.

'No more Chopin tonight,' she said, in between his firm kisses, and, laughing at this, they walked hand-in-hand into the bedroom, with its rectangular poster bed from the eighteenth century and custom-made mattresses from the present.

The first few times they made love, they did so very carefully, as if they were physically disabled or blind and risked bumping hard into each other; it was dark in the bedroom. Yet even during their unlit delights, Karl could tell that Una's body wasn't the same as it once had been. Her belly had assumed other forms, and he didn't recognize her breasts as the same ones. They were bigger, and slightly droopy. It was a disappointment that he felt physically; it actually left a bitter taste in his mouth. At the same time, he blamed himself for this situation. That her breasts wouldn't have turned out like this if they had been in his care, and he paid them special attention as compensation for their mistreatment and neglect.

All seven of their days in Beauséjour, they generally didn't fall asleep until morning, not wanting sleep to separate them. They would sit up for a little while, exchange one more kiss, have a sip of water, lie down and embrace each other from tip to toe, make love partly and fully, seriously or frolicsomely, have a new glass of red wine before bed, go to the bathroom, nibble on almonds, brush their teeth again, take another shower, listen to "Two Sleepy People" one more time, and whisper like naughty children who can always come up with a way to prolong their fun—and certainly not go to sleep.

When they did finally sleep, they held hands, as if they were walking hand-in-hand in the forest or on a sandy beach. They slept late into the day, like a little brother and sister who had been separated from their parents in a fog on a heath, suffered there through the night and finally fell asleep exhausted at daybreak.

Karl Ástuson, who, from a Tuesday morning following Merchants' Weekend when he was nineteen years old, until one February night many, many years later, had no idea what the future meant, now settled into the future. At the same time as he tried with all his might to make each moment whole and perfect in itself, he waited for it to pass, so that he could start reminiscing on how Una's eye sparkled when he softly revealed to her that he had thought about her, always; never lost sight of her for one single day that God had given him—yet had never imagined that the days would come that now were here. That it took him time, when he stirred and woke from his night's sleep, to realize that this wasn't a dream: Una is here, life is here, in this earthly paradise close to Arles.

But they really didn't talk much that first week. Perhaps they were taking a rest after all the unspoken words through the long years when Karl and Una were surrounded by each other's silence, as if dead in spirit. When they conversed, they felt their way slowly onward with their words, as if they were practicing a new language and didn't want to make any grammatical errors.

In the absence of words, they listened to music incessantly; in the car, in the conservatory, in the bedroom. They slept to music and woke to music, and made it themselves. On this point, Una was demanding, and forced Karl to play more music than he liked. She hadn't forgotten the story of the composer Karl Ástuson, and he was compelled to recall the *Yes-tango* that he had written, both lyrics and notes.

This tango was premiered on Ástamama's birthday. Karl thought of how he lay in bed in the evenings, listening to long strings of yesyesses and yeseyesyesyesses coming up from the living room as the sewing machine sped along, and it crossed his mind to surprise his mother on her birthday by coming up with a tango for Yes—for piano, violin, clarinet, sewing machine, and soprano.

The piece began with a very soft note from the clarinet, followed by notes from the violin, with one tiny yes, supported by the piano. Then a string of Yesses was born, and the sewing machine (in actuality, a soulless noisemaker) was used as a percussive instrument. Now high yesses multiplied, but were, in the end, outweighed by the clarinet and violin, jubilant and noisy, along with the piano. Then everything went quiet, until the soprano sang a decisive 'Yes!' And the sewing machine hummed down to its final rattle.

When Una was finally done applauding the performance of this one-man orchestra, Karl told her that his mother had bid farewell to this world with this word on her lips. This was one of the things that were too sad to tell Una once upon a time. And now, for the first time, he described how his mother had uttered one crystal-clear 'yes,' before she died, as a young woman might have said when she went out the door, perhaps on her way downtown, and was reminding herself of an errand that she absolutely mustn't forget.

On the other hand, he didn't say anything about the little girl's sweater that his mother occupied herself with knitting after she fell ill, a sweater that was always there in a battered suitcase in the music room on Long Island. It was entirely uncertain whether he would ever show her the sweater and tell her that Ástamama had given her regards to the little girl that he wanted to have.

She wasn't on the agenda now, the sweater-girl; no children were. Una said nothing about why she didn't have a child, and he didn't want to pry. He pushed aside the thought that their own child might come into being some day, maybe even now, immediately, or that Una might not be able to have a child. He didn't ask if he should take precautions, and he didn't. He had no idea what was going on in Una's mind, whether she'd been on the pill since last time, and she gave nothing away.

In the landscape of many unspoken words, the two travelers knew each other as well as if they'd passed through the centuries of reincarnation together—so well, in fact, that they weren't even surprised at how many things they no longer shared in common. For instance, how their taste in restaurants was now different. A detail that had hardly ever come into play in their former life.

Now it turned out that Una was most fond of ugly little places with ordinary food. She didn't understand why food was supposed to look like a Japanese flower arrangement, and felt most at home in a truck stop restaurant with a buffet by Country Road 113. There, however, Karl felt like a man on the run, and looked around guiltily while filling his plate, as if he'd been caught red-handed in a crime. A man who generally didn't dine at restaurants with less than at least one Michelin star, and who scrutinized the wine list like a biologist with an abnormal specimen under his microscope. The wine didn't matter to Una—only that it didn't taste bad. Yes, she liked a good wine, but such a thing should preferably be drunk at home; it was always far too expensive in restaurants.

As far as attire went, there had previously been little separating Karl and Una. The best-dressed couple at school, both of them an only child, and he in homemade clothing that appeared tailored by the finest designers. Now he wore nothing but designer labels. Una, on the other hand, wasn't one for paying exorbitantly for clothing, and on top of that, had decided that clothing and shoes should be comfortable—not constrictive. She was none too pleased when Karl decided to buy her high-heeled shoes, and when he brought her the shoes to try on, she gave him a withering look—as if he were trying to squeeze her into a Dirndl because he found it sexy. Toward the end of their week in Paradise, Karl and Una remembered that people's lives aren't just music and kisses, but are also full of so-called facts. Even if these things seemed irrelevant, it was probably a good idea to take them into account when starting a new life.

Had she completed her degree in solo piano? What was her Master's thesis in Italian about? When did she stop working at the Icelandic Opera? What year did she move to Silfurströnd? What were her favorite places in Italy? What was she invariably doing there?

Una asked about the house on Long Island, which she thought was the most exciting house in the world besides her own beloved funkis house, and she questioned him in detail about Lotta. Karl felt instinctively that the situation would be awkward, and he immediately made plans to keep the two women apart. To remove his office from his house and rent an office space within walking distance. That was logical, in the same way that you don't put two sopranos together on stage.

Una knew that Karl was a businessman, but what kind of business?, she asked on day four, as they were having their morning coffee in the conservatory, even if it wasn't morning as such, since it was now two o'clock.

'That's the thing,' he said. 'I'm a speculator of the incomprehensible variety. Partygoers tend to flee when my livelihood comes up in conversation.'

'Does this incomprehensible speculation have a name?' she asked.

And it did have a name. Karl Ástuson belonged to an elite group whose profession was known as *arbitreur* in French. Their business was called *arbitrage*.

'Abracadabra,' said Una. 'Explain, please.'

'The idea is to identify price differentials and profit from them. For instance in the exchange rate of a currency from one country to the next; buying and selling at the right moment. I could also find a stock of one hundred Mercedes Benzes at a good price in Timbuktu and sell them at a higher price in Nicaragua. Or vice versa. Hocus Pocus.'

'So, speculation to a higher degree,' said Una. 'You focus on differences—which makes you a discriminator.'

'Ah—you've hit it on the nose.'

'You can't discriminate when it comes to me.'

'I've always discriminated when it comes to you, ever since we were eleven years old. I've always put you first, ever since I first saw you. I'm never going to stop doing so.'

Una looked at the man and said nothing. They both sat lost in thought until a stray dove landed on the roof and cut the silence with its prolonged, bluesy cooing.

Then Una said: 'Discrimination to a higher degree.'

They laughed, and then fell silent again, until Una said: 'I want to join you in the speculation business. Such elation we would share—in combined speculation.'

They giggled about this lame attempt at a joke all evening, and poked fun at each other with it: elation ... speculation ... speculelation.

However, Karl wasn't about to bring Una into the speculation business. Her place was at the grand piano on Long Island. (A Bösendorfer, of course, like the Music College. A softer sound than in a Steinway.) Yes, she was allowed to read books in between.

'Hmph, you don't have any books,' she said.

'Yes I do have books, loads of them; including in Icelandic. Some from my mom. But I have even have more sheet music. An entire room full of sheet music.'

He could hardly believe his own ears. He had finally shared his secret, just like that: a music room, with all that was in it. No one was allowed in there, not even Immaculata. He cleaned and dusted this room himself, once a week, happily.

'An entire room?'

'Yes. Not a small one, either. Now I'll have to add a chair, actually; it only has one armchair. But what of that? You don't have to lift a finger. Not up for discussion.'

'It wouldn't bother me to have to lift a finger. I painted the entire top floor at Silfurströnd. Alone.'

'Was your husband that stingy?'

'No, I'm the one who's stingy. Besides, I find painting so enjoyable.'

'You'll have no need for stinginess if it's up to me.'

'It won't be.'

'I'd forgotten that I've never been married. I guess that's the way marriages work.'

'To be more precise, the woman's in charge of all the small details, and the man of the big ones,' said Una.

'I'll keep that in mind,' said Karl.

A constant cause for astonishment that week in Beauséjour was how Karl and Una, who were, strictly speaking, strangers, would help each other out with everything as if they had been teamed up all their lives. What was difficult for one, was easy for the other. They complemented each other. That's how it had always been—take, for example, German and mathematics—but it wasn't a given that this would hold up when it came down to cooking a beef stew from a local recipe so many years later that neither had any inclination to think back on all the time they'd been apart.

They were so ridiculously well-coordinated, literally, that they could still play the piano together, four-handed, without making any mistakes to speak of. That was an old talent, but they also discovered a new one, per se: acting as co-authors of short fiction for the world in the form of text messages about Una's journey—and their future, supposedly chance meeting in New York. It was another matter whether this version would be readily and fully believed. The main thing was to stick with it.

One thief, and only one, managed to break into their Paradise. It was a brainless animal, the notorious wetland mosquito, which bit Una and made her eye sink beneath a swollen mound. This occurred on day five, when they went to the seaside village of Saintes-Maries-de-la-Mer.

Una was wondering about the name; here three Saint Mary's (according to the guidebook) had arrived by boat. She had only ever heard of Saint Mary in the singular—she who was so well versed in art history, and a regular at the galleries in Florence and Venice. And Karl began thinking of the many Mary's in his life: Ástamama, Sigríður, Doreen Ash, Lotta ... his half-sister Fríða, yes ...

'What are you thinking about?' asked Una, when she noticed the Mary-look on Karl's face.

'I think mostly about you.'

'You don't have to. I'm with you.'

'I'm sorry to be so unpractical, but I still think about you, even if you're with me. And you've been bitten right by your eye.'

There was nothing else for the happiest people in the world to do but rush to Arles and seek medical attention.

It was awkward. When Karl Ástuson walked in with a woman with a swollen eye, a doctor and nurse both looked at him as if he were a wife beater.

'They think I hit you,' he said, in a slightly worried tone.

'Let them,' said Una in an obstinate tone, like a woman who'd been beaten, without it being anyone's concern but hers.

Karl and Una never went back to Beauséjour, not even to pick their green and purple olives in the autumn. Before the year was out, they sold the little eighteenth century castle to a man they'd never seen, and whose name they didn't even know, because Lotta arranged the sale. In its place, they bought a new palace, a new Paradise on the French side between the Pyrenees and a beach. It was called Beaulieu, and there they experienced new dreamtimes. Also there, Karl told a tale that Una had heard twice before, in Beauséjour and Reykjavík.

The girl behind the screen

Once upon a time there was an eleven-year-old boy who lived in a corner house in the center of town, with his mother who was a seamstress, incredibly musical, and his half-sister, who was also somewhat musical. He himself played the piano in the living room, and that was in fact what he was doing one snowy day in the run up to Christmas. In this corner house, the mother did her sewing in the living room behind an oriental folding screen, while her only son practiced playing the piano—and by this point, he had become quite adept at this noble instrument. This particular winter's day, the son of the seamstress was completely absorbed in his Chopin and didn't notice anything until suddenly, there on the carpet was a warmly-dressed girl with a snowflake on her woolen cap, probably the same age as he—which she in fact turned out to be.

The young piano player was so startled by this sight that he got up and began heading toward the kitchen, thinking it would be best not to be in the way if she were trying on a Christmas dress, and that he could get himself a glass of milk. But then this miracle occurred, which was, all things considered, the greatest miracle in his life, before or since. The girl spoke to him in a low voice that would doubtless develop into a mezzo-soprano over time, saying: 'Keep playing.' This left the young boy flabbergasted; he felt his heart race and looked into the kindly face of his mother for reassurance that the girl's request wasn't completely unreasonable. His mother then stated, in her familiar frank manner: 'You're not at all in our way.'

So the son continued to play, making a few mistakes at the start, since this newcomer made him shy. But Chopin with his Valse de l'adieu, The Farewell Waltz, soon gained the upper hand, and now the boy played as never before. He became so engrossed in the music that he completely forgot time and place, and finally stood up without realizing the fitting taking place in the same room. Which led to him witnessing when the Christmas dress slipped over the girl, giving him a glimpse of her bare knee and the toes of one foot, for the girl didn't take enough care to ensure that she was completely hidden by the screen. The boy was tremendously startled by this sight, but managed to hide it and walked calmly into the kitchen as if nothing had happened. Nor could he tell if the girl had noticed anything.

In the kitchen, he got himself his intended glass of milk and some crumbled cookies that he'd recently bought directly from the factory, and he recalled very clearly that the girl in the living room had short, dark hair and slightly tan skin. He also recalled that the Christmas dress was made from exceptionally red velvet (so red that it seemed to him more like crimson) and that the dress had a white-lace bodice and velvet-covered buttons. He was sitting there on a kitchen stool, with a glass of milk and a rapidly beating heart, when the girl, dressed for the weather once more, walked past the kitchen door and bade him a soft goodbye with a cheerful smile.

He was so disoriented by this visit that he stood for some time as if dumbfounded at the kitchen door, and the dance teacher named Jón, who had just arrived, was so amused by the sight of the seamstress's son in the doorway, in such a state and holding a cookie, that he said 'Bon appetit' as he walked into the living room.

That same evening, the son in the corner house learned from his mother that the girl was named Una, and that she too was learning to play the piano. She was the only child of rather elderly parents, and lived on Grundarstígur. Her father was a merchant. Upon further inquiry, he also discovered that her house was a corner house like his—and he thought a great deal about this divine providence.

There was much more about the girl that he found enormously interesting, and it didn't help when, at a far too tender age, he made Boris Pasternak's Doctor Zhivago his Christmas reading—everything in this novel revolves around Yuri's love for Lara. He decided to call the girl behind the screen Una Lara, and began thinking about studying medicine.

In short, the girl with the short hair fixed herself in his memory, as did the miracle of her, when she said: 'Keep playing.' As time passed, he kept an eye on her; for instance, while ice-skating on the Pond or on other occasions, and when, following a New Year's bonfire in high school, they became sweethearts, he felt like he was in seventh heaven.

Could he now finally ask Una the question that he'd been pondering ever since he was eleven years old: 'Why did you, having been raised so well, come into the living room wearing your coat?' And the answer was obvious: 'The doorbell didn't work.'

The Good Lover

'Why didn't you tell me she was black?'

'I've never said she was white.'

'You can't wriggle your way out. Discriminator.'

Then they laughed, yet even so, Una felt disappointed, as if Karl had kept something important from her. Nothing less than the skin color of his right hand, who had just retreated into her office following her first polite conversation with the new woman of the house.

Karl had bought himself some time by sending Lotta on a two-week holiday the day before he and Una arrived in America. What for? he asked himself; it hardly altered the situation into which he had maneuvered himself. Come what may, instead of planning things out like a man, taking imme-diate steps to move the office out of the house and having the ingenuity to inform Una about important points, such as skin color, even if such things were irrelevant to him.

Now he tried to make up for his errors laying all his cards on the table. He spoke about Lotta and their entire relationship for twelve whole minutes, with all the rhetorical finesse he'd learned on his high-school Debate team. Among other things, it surfaced that her parents had been human-rights advocates; that Lotta had prophesied that the next president of the USA would be colored and that she thought she knew who it would be even if he wasn't yet widely known.

'Does she read tea leaves, as well?'

'Don't underestimate Lotta.'

'I don't. And she's in love with you.'

'How could she not be? I'm irresistible.'

'This isn't a joke.'

'Is it a joke that I'm irresistible?'

'Cut it out. She's in love with you.'

'She can be anything she wants; it's not my fault. And I'm going to find an office space nearby.'

'Move the problem to the next street.'

'Better than having it here,' said he.

Now Una wanted to know whether Karl had followed the basic principle of keeping his work and private lives separate, or if he had slept with Lotta. When Karl said no, it still wasn't enough—had he wanted to?

'What do you take me for? Of course I wanted to.'

'Of course you did. She's stunning,' said Una jealously.

'That's not the point. What matters is that I don't have a crush on her, and never have. In such matters, I'm very single-minded, as you well know.'

'Yes, I know,' said Una, smiling a combination of her wonderful smile and her mischievous smile (a new variation, and particularly charming) and putting an end to the awkwardness for now, except when she asked him if he didn't find it funny that Lotta should call him master.

Yes, he thought it was.

Why did he find it funny?

'Just because,' said Karl.

'It isn't just because, don't you understand? She's descended from slaves. You're a white master and she's a colored slave.'

'She isn't paid a slave's wages,' said Karl—and he felt terribly ashamed, having missed this irony.

Fear of losing respect in Una's eyes flared up inside him. And he saw in a flash that that was how it would be even if they were ninety. He would never feel entirely sure whether he was doing the right thing—whether he might somehow offend Una and perhaps risk alienating her. This whole thing represented a fundamental change in his existence, particularly since he had been more or less at ease the past seventeen years. It's so easy when nothing matters enough to act neurotic about it.

Karl Ástuson tried to make up for his embarrassing blunder by immediately tackling the Lotta Case with the precision of a structural engineer. He moved his office to the next street. He came up with new rules concerning communication and interaction with his private secretary. This involved two things: showing her less attention and more attention at the same time. Giving her flowers, which he hadn't ever done before on a regular basis, and raising her salary, which he hadn't done until now without her asking him to do so. On the other hand, he spent a lot less time with her, working mainly from home, but meeting with her daily to go over assignments and financial details.

Lotta took all of these changes in her stride, a professional to her fingertips. It was impossible to tell if she was pleased with the changes or not. She was, however, less cheerful than usual. She lost weight and began wearing clothing in more muted tones. Karl took these changes in Lotta personally: the Lotta who had assisted him so conscientiously and faithfully in reaching his goals, and as such, had helped pave the way toward his main goal: regaining Una. He hoped for her sake that she would make a decision: either to quit, or to come to terms with the new circumstances, but she did neither. There was nothing he could do to help but behave even more respectably, in both word and deed, than he was used to, so as not to hurt the woman with a new variety of heartbreak, any more than he already had.

Even with the distraction of Lotta and other things, they shored up their existence and each other; Karl and Una, continuously harmonious and good-spirited, in the house from where they had a partial view of the capital of the world. They scraped together as large a dose of dreamtime as was possible: by turning off their phones or letting them ring out; by taking daily walks on one of the beaches, no matter the weather, and gathering pebble after pebble; by attending concerts and losing themselves in the moment; by making trips to the countryside and finding a place to stay that could have been the backdrop to eternity; that is, by a frozen lake beneath evergreen trees that swayed like dancers with numerous arms and legs.

Living together with Una was like living underwater. Every day brought a new kind of lightness, a weightlessness that only love brings forth, and to Karl, it seemed as if he were floating, or at least barely touching the ground. Una mentioned that he had become unusually light on his feet. Without a hint of irony. He was in fact still losing weight, and his taste in food had changed. In his hermit life, Karl Ástuson had eaten steaks with salad and drunk red wine. Whiskeys in between. With Una, he ate fish and shellfish, and drank mainly champagne and white wine. He laid off the whiskey.

By the time spring on Long Island had run its course and it was clear that summer would develop without any setbacks, Una and Karl had gained control of the distractions and veiled the house on Long Island from the outer world in such a way that it could not get in, except according to fixed rules—and it was totally excluded from the music room, where, if needed, they often listened to one fine aria in particular: *Happy We*, by Handel, and at worst sang along.

But at the start of the summer with Una, and in the special joy that comes with summer in general, not to mention when we're in love, Karl was about to discover that he existed in a dimension beyond Una—and that there, another woman had settled.

In other words, this precise man began to notice, to his dismay, soon after he and Una had rooted themselves on Long Island, that his mind was revolving slowly and surely around Doreen Ash. What on earth was his steadfast mind doing there?

His debt of gratitude had been paid in writing, with well-chosen words that had taken a long time to formulate. It wasn't enough; nothing was, when the debt was so huge. But to catch oneself in the act of thinking about a benefactress, time and time again? To be obsessed with her—or what? It was so abysmal that he would have scourged himself with a cat-o'-nine-tails if he'd believed this method could help rid his mind of this pest.

Karl Ástuson's thoughts swirled so persistently around Doreen Ash that he dared not sit idly by. He couldn't risk anything that might ruin things for him and Una. He thought hard about what on earth he could do about this, and the only thing he could think of was: 'Go and meet Doreen.' See if he could curb his thoughts on this woman, rein them in and sort them into tidy piles, like papers on a desk.

It would be natural to visit her under the pretext of gratitude. He selected a generous gift for his savior, a platinum bracelet set with lapis lazuli. This, too, seemed natural—but why did he have *From Karl* engraved on the inside? He told himself that he was instilling the gift with something extra. But did he really believe this? Shouldn't he have paid some consideration to her jealous partner? Liina something, with two *i*-s, the psychologist?

He took the train to New York, which was highly unusual. He hadn't announced his coming (also highly unusual), and as he sat there by the train window, in his highly unusual state of mind, the big city opened its arms to him, with all that was to be found therein—and in particular, a lover: Doreen Ash. A life-giving midwife whom one would never guess to be so from appearances. She was rather more off-putting than attractive, and would likely have never described herself first as a 'good person.' Yet upon closer inspection, her goodness became apparent; much more so than in those people who wrap themselves in a mild veil of graciousness and say: 'Here's good old me!'

Doreen Ash had an office a few minutes away from the zoo in Central Park, Karl's favorite spot in the city that had acted as his stepmother during his college years, held him in her cool embrace when he started working at a bank and began to get his feet under him. He had enjoyed wandering about the zoo, looking at the monkeys and snakes and penguins, in order to lose himself in the moment, to stop feeling sad for a time, stop feeling helpless, a very young man who had eternally lost what was dearest to him, Una and Ástamama.

It must have been Doreen Ash who answered the door phone when he said his name, because he wasn't asked what he wanted; instead, he was let in without a word.

Karl was surprised to see Doreen Ash waiting at the elevator door on the seventh floor, and even more surprised to see that she'd aged more than the three years that had passed since they saw each other last. He kissed her on the cheek. She didn't move, didn't blink. Received the kiss like a sentry. Yet she did lay her finger on the back of his hand, so lightly and fleetingly that it was hardly a touch—puzzling, and not at all like Doreen Ash.

Her office, her consulting room, was also not at all like Doreen Ash as he saw her. If he were to have guessed how she arranged and decorated her consulting room, he would have said: Pristine modern design. Chrome and white. Yet the room was quite the opposite: dark colors, brown and burgundy, a dark parquet floor, old leather furniture, including a Freudian couch, and a big old oak desk. African masks on the wall. Egyptian cat on a desk. A view over the zoo, that historical site from his past life in the city, where, however, nothing had really happened apart from him regaining some sense of his *joie de vivre*. As much as was possible without Una.

Doreen Ash sat down behind the desk, and Karl Ástuson opposite her. Like a client. A patient. They said nothing. On the other hand, faint animal sounds from the zoo were carried in through the open window.

'I was hoping you'd come, and you've come at a good time,' said Doreen Ash finally, without being asked if this was a convenient time.

'I'm glad to hear that,' said Karl. 'Of course, I couldn't have known if you were busy with patients.'

'I'm gradually reducing the amount of patients I see, but there are two that I'll apparently be treating until death do us part. I don't know if it's me who can't free myself from them, or they from me, but that's how it is. Both men, of course. Typical mommy's boys and closeted homosexuals; what else. One of them still lives with his mother, even, but he's only forty-one. I still haven't figured out which one of them is holding tighter to the other, the mom to him, or him to her. Even though he's been coming to me for seven years. I guess I'm not meant to get to the bottom of this one; and anyway, I don't believe it's possible to get to the truth about people.'

'Strange.'

'If you want to get to the truth about a particular person, you can search for a long time.'

'So what is it you do at work, then?'

'Well, I'm actually quitting.'

'Because the truth about a person is too inaccessible?'

'It might not really matter that the truth is complicated or obscure. You can create a working model of a person's life, a copy that's hopefully not too far from the original. Now, if this model helps a person find his way through life, that's better than nothing.'

'So therapy involves building models?'

'In my experience, yes. Models of things we don't have clear ideas about. It's like working in a fog. Groping blindly in the dark.'

'You're not the only one who's described his work like that. A writer did, too, if I remember correctly.'

'The blind are apt at finding their way.'

'Okay.'

'The truth aside, it's healthy and good and normal to discuss one's problems with a so-called neutral party. Someone who is not a friend and not a family member. A therapist isn't really neutral, of course—or at least I don't try to imagine that I am. I'm just objective in a different way than a friend or family member. And I take the burden off of friends and families. My patients are free to turn to more pleasant subjects after they unburdened themselves with me.'

'As I seem to recall, patients get on your nerves.'

'Only those who have real issues. Those who are in their own world and repeat the same egomaniacal bullshit year after year. It's torture, listening to it.'

'But aren't you specially trained not to take personally what people say?'

'What kind of training do you think could prepare you for that? And the ones who appear to be completely out of touch with the world always have a special knack for slipping in behind your defenses.'

They fell silent and he gazed at his savior, the woman who had aged ten years in the space of three. Maybe she was destroying herself with alcohol, as she'd implied. Thick cheeks, swollen eyelids. And it looked as if she'd developed an immobile Humphrey Bogart upper lip, one of the surefire symptoms.

It wasn't just that time hadn't been kind to Doreen Ash; she actually seemed like a different woman. There was a melancholy hanging over her that hadn't been there when they first met. Maybe she'd lost a close friend or relative.

She was also dressed very differently than the night he met her. Then, she wore a casual summer dress, white. It was a wrap dress that hadn't proven an obstacle when it came time for business. Now she had on a red Chanel dress suit, and looked more like a businesswoman then a psychiatrist. Karl caught himself counting the golden, spherical buttons on the jacket; there were eleven. Such a garment would be more than a nuisance if it came to undressing the woman, and the tight skirt formed its own special barrier. He vaguely recalled an awkward moment when a lover of his was wearing an extremely tight, inaccessible garment, and he'd had quite a lot of trouble removing it. Their game very nearly degenerated into a scuffle.

'Any news about your new book?'

'They'll soon start promoting it—not tomorrow or the day after, but the day after that.'

'Congratulations.'

'Too soon, but thanks. Still, it's predicted to be a bestseller, but I guess I've already told you.'

'Great.'

'Predictions don't always come true.'

'What's the name of the book?'

Doreen Ash laughed and said: 'You'll see soon enough.'

'Oh?'

'It's important that it remains a secret until the last moment.'

'I'll buy a copy as soon it hits the stores,' said Karl Ástuson.

'I'll send you a signed copy,' said Doreen Ash, before adding dryly: 'Are you still living in the same place?'

'Yes, thanks,' said Karl Ástuson, who preferred not to be reminded of their meeting at his house. He hurriedly took out the present.

The box with the bracelet was wrapped artfully in white Japanese paper and decorated with a pink porcelain flower. How inappropriate this packaging was. It resembled a wedding present, though no one was getting married. The saleswoman had apparently assumed it was for his fiancée, and he had made no attempt to stop her misguided gift-wrapping.

It was almost like trying to solve a Rubik's cube, unwrapping this present that the saleswoman had expertly prepared and tied with filigree threads. And Doreen Ash's hands weren't entirely steady. They both remained silent until the bracelet was unwrapped.

'Exquisite bracelet,' she said. 'Thank you. This is far too much.'

She didn't try it on, but held it up and looked closely at it and its deep blue stones with gold veins.

'Nothing's too much. You saved me. And Una as well. Horrible marriage. She was married to a control freak. A wife beater, probably. I think she's too proud to talk about it.'

'Are you planning to have a child?'

'What?'

'A child?'

'I haven't thought about it.'

'Has she?'

'We don't talk about children. She never had a child in her long marriage, and children are pretty much like aliens to me. Except that I was close to a little niece of mine, a long time ago.'

'What if the woman got pregnant?'

'Then we would have a baby. It's no more complex than that. Unless she would prefer an abortion.'

117

'Hold on, now.'

'I can't see inside people's heads, I don't read minds, I can't know what Una is thinking unless she tells me.'

'You've come so far as to understand the basics.'

'Thanks for the compliment. Actually, it's I who should be complimenting you—you saved my life, literally. It was so empty that I could just as well have been dead.'

'Rescue missions are usually a lost cause. Unbelievable that your story was a success. I really can't get over it. The key thing is that I'm not your doctor. If I were, I wouldn't have been allowed to talk to you as I did. If I had been your doctor, I wouldn't have been able to do anything so revolutionary for you. I wish that I could do something similar for my two oddments. Hopeless cases that I'm stuck with, and they with me, like a sculpture representing hopelessness—the best thing you can say is better than nothing, but it isn't good enough. And then there's me—who is supposed to save me? I obviously can't, or won't. Not even Liina can save me. I actually think that I hold onto my two hopeless cases, my eternal mama's boys, like a lifeline. It's unprofessional; against all the rules. Of course, since I realize this, I should get rid of them—yet I don't.'

Karl Ástuson didn't know what to say, so he said nothing, according to his mother's repeated instruction: *If you don't know what to say, it's best to say nothing.*

He said nothing for so long that Doreen Ash repeated: 'Yes, who is supposed to save me?' Then she put on the bracelet of platinum and lapis lazuli, the gift from Karl, and looked at her wrist as if she were looking at a watch, but still couldn't tell what time it was.

'Is there anything I can do?' he asked, thinking at the same time how silly it sounded.

'You least of all,' said Doreen, with her eyes still on the bracelet.

Karl Ástuson looked her in the face, but it gave no indication of why he, least of all, could do something for her. All he could do was repeat it: 'Least of all me.'

'You know that I'm in love with you,' she said.

There was no emphasis in the sentence; it was devoid of all energy. Almost as if she'd been saying: 'You know we're out of potatoes.'

'What nonsense,' he said. 'You're more into women.'

Doreen Ash burst out laughing and said ever so sweetly, almost as if she were talking to a little puppy: 'Mama's boy.'

'I had a mom who was so wonderful that it's practically incomprehensible. Everything around her was life and color, warmth and laughter. The childhood she created for me was a dream and fairytale. If I hadn't had this mother, I would never have believed in dreams and fairytales—I would never have managed to cross a seventeen-year-long bridge and start a new life, out of sheer luck. And if that makes me a mama's boy, then I'm going to be one until I die.'

A look of admiration came over Doreen Ash's face—she'd never seen Karl Ástuson get upset. He was slightly startled to see this expression on the woman who said she was in love with him. Was it possible? Was this a trap to get him in bed?

'It's cocktail hour,' said Doreen Ash. 'What can I get you?'

'Do you have gin and tonic?' he asked—he who no longer indulged in distilled spirits.

Doreen Ash fetched the necessary ingredients from a piece of furniture that looked like a file cabinet, but was in fact a refrigerator.

'This is my secret,' she said. 'Not even Liina knows about it. No one except the cleaning lady. It's also she who keeps it stocked, and removes the empties. Otherwise, my life is so trivial that I have no other secrets. Apart from you, of course. Because you're a secret. And certainly not a trivial one. Big enough that I've told no one about you, and don't intend to, either.'

She wasn't going to yield on this. As the smitten Doreen Ash mixed two exceptionally strong gin and tonics, Karl Ástuson figuratively spat in his palms and prepared himself for continued conversation with her. This situation irritated him. He had bought a ridiculously expensive bracelet for her as a token of his gratitude. He went to her because he didn't understand why she was so much in his way, and was hoping to get some answers. Now he was even further than before from getting to the bottom of this. And what was worse—now she would be doubly in his way. A woman who was head over heels in love.

How was he to handle this? Who would have thought that a savior and angel of destiny could start making trouble when it had accomplished its mission? It should just have gone its way, quietly. But this one didn't know how to, and got so tangled up between its protégé's legs that he lost his balance and fell flat on his back at the feet of his savior, his arms and legs waving like an upside-down fly's.

It was obvious that he'd laid a trap for himself by going to see Doreen Ash. As if someone once said, so insightfully: 'We're specialists at laying traps for ourselves.' He would have liked to discuss this topic particularly with Doreen Ash, but she probably wasn't the right person to talk to about this sticky, hidden trap he'd walked into, because she was the trap, in the flesh.

She sat back down in the chair at her desk and they touched glasses. She took a big drink, shook her head, and said, as if amused by some nonsense of her own: 'I realized it when you smiled at me—remember, on the sidewalk outside your house when I wouldn't let you pay for the taxi. That's when I realized it. Like I'd been hit on the head. It had never happened to me before.'

'You must have fallen in love before.'

'Not like this. Before, it was with people I'd known and spent time with. It took time. This just happened, just like that. I also know when it happened. It happened when you said, outside the bar: "Just as well it wasn't rainbows." Remember?'

Her tone, truth be told, had grown accusatory. As if the man she was talking to could do something about this. That he'd actually said that about rainbows in order to set a heartbreaking destiny in motion. Or that this situation, this infatuation, could have been prevented if he hadn't gone and added rainbows to the mix.

'I don't get it. You told me on the phone that I'd scared you away from men for good.'

'It became so obvious when I met you how hopeless this is. In you I'd found a perfectly likeable man and dream lover, whom I fell in love with immediately. And at whom I had no shot at all.'

'How could you have known that?'

'I sometimes see things very clearly, and I can occasionally stop myself, if I do so early enough.'

'What was so clear?'

'That you could never fall in love with me.'

'Hold on a second. I can't fall in love with anyone. I have only one true love. There are no others.'

'There, you see.'

'Yes, but it's impossible to take me as a measuring stick. Have you ever met anyone like me?'

'It wouldn't have changed anything even if I'd known exactly why I couldn't have you. I just knew that it would never work. I would never have considered making a pass at you, any more than with a gay person.'

'But what about Liina?'

'What about Liina?'

'You must be in love with her.'

'Are you nuts? It's she who's been after me for longer than I care to remember. She adores me, the poor girl. After I met you, I thought to myself that she would finally get her reward, which is actually pretty questionable. Liina has been my right hand; without her I could never have written such a book. She even wrote drafts for more than one of the scientific chapters. And it's she who takes care of the daily details: the bills and car, all that stuff. I'm not particularly proud of being in such a mistress-and-servant sort of relationship. It isn't love with a big "L," as I would have wanted. But it was my chance not to be alone. To have someone to cuddle with. I've never met anyone else that I could even come close to imagining living with. It's comfortable living with Liina, and it's not boring, but maybe not particularly fun, either. Nothing is particularly fun, so to speak. My life has no content apart from love, and the sadness of not being able to experience love except in my mind. That's the content of my life now, apart from anything else.'

'I would never have dreamed of suggesting that you elope with Anja unless I was in love with you. I wouldn't have had the energy to boss you as I did, or any interest in doing so, either, unless I was in love with you. The fact that the whole thing worked is a comfort to me, in spite of it all. A painkiller; ointment on my wounds. I feel somewhat better, or I suffer less, because I gave you the chance to have something you can call a life. I don't call it a life if it doesn't have any emotional content. When love is unrequited, it becomes so piercingly clear how much is missing. Then it dawns on you that life can be the purest dance on roses, but that you simply don't have that option—it has been taken from you, and life as it is becomes small and ugly compared to the big, bright life that could be, if there were love in it. I guess you know better than anyone what I'm talking about.'

'Better than anyone, I don't know. But I understand.'

'It's endlessly painful to see you sitting here so close to me,' said Doreen Ash. 'But it's also beautiful.'

'I'm just an ordinary man,' said Karl Ástuson, breaking his mother's rule about saying nothing, if there was any doubt about what to say. And he added: 'There's nothing special about me. Remember that.'

'That's what you think. Not only are you unusual, you're also downright mysterious. You've never told me why you were so startled when you saw my business card. Did you think you'd slept with your half-sister?'

For the rest of his life, Karl Ástuson was proud of answering, like an actor performing his seventy-first show: 'As I told you, I have a half-sister named Fríða. I can tell you two apart.'

Doreen Ash laughed, and Karl Ástuson saw that he might not have a better opportunity to escape. He stood up, dignified, and asked: 'Will I see you again?'

Doreen Ash said nothing, and didn't stir. Then she smiled suddenly, and said: 'I have an idea. Not tomorrow, but the day after, my book is being published, and the publisher is holding a party. Would you like to come? This one time.'

'Yes, thank you. Of course I'll come.'

'Could you do me a favor and not come with a woman?'

'Certainly,' he said. 'I owe you as much.'

'You're funny,' she said, and neither of them laughed.

She reached across the massive oak desk and handed him an invitation.

Karl Ástuson felt like Doreen Ash's third oddment, as she called them. Surely she had handed both of them invitations across the desk, the two mama's boys, the patients from whom she couldn't tear herself, or they from her—the same ones who couldn't tear themselves from their mothers, or they from them.

'Did they also get invitations, the other two?' he asked.

123

'As a matter of fact, they did,' said Doreen Ash. 'But there's no comparison.'

She walked him to the elevator, but made no move to say goodbye to him other than with a handshake. He hugged her tightly and kissed her on the cheek. This time she bowed her head just a touch. He felt her breath against the skin of his neck, the warmth from his life-giver's breathing.

'Thanks,' she then said, in a neutral voice.

'It's I who should be thanking you. Always.'

'See you day after tomorrow,' she said.

'I look forward to it.'

The elevator was on its way up, and Doreen Ash hesitated. As soon as it arrived, she said: 'There is one thing.'

'Yes,' said Karl Ástuson, preparing for the worst.

'In the unlikely event that you meet Liina, I haven't told her anything other than that we met by coincidence and had dinner together a few years ago. That you then phoned me and I helped you out of a pinch. It's best if we tell the same story.'

'Of course,' said Karl Ástuson, with a smile. 'In the unlikely event.'

Without cracking a smile, Doreen Ash opened the elevator door, and at that, he left.

There was no denying that Karl Ástuson put special effort into his appearance and clothing before attending Doreen's publication party, celebrating a book with a title that was a secret until the last moment. He ended up having a facial massage, manicure, and haircut at a salon that Lotta had found for him, in a custom-made chair with a view over the harbor. The client was not allowed to move from the chair the entire two hours he was being pampered.

He felt as if an important event were in the offing, and admitted to himself that he was as nervous as he'd sometimes been before meeting Una in the old days. As if he mustn't rush into anything, had to put more effort than usual into everything he did. That was the burden Ástamama had laid on his shoulders; she wanted him to be perfect, and said that he was perfect. Which meant that he couldn't allow himself to be anything less than that, and did everything with finesse: having coffee, putting on his shoes, signing a check.

And now there was a question of whether the man who wanted to do everything right should buy flowers for a savior who was just about to publish a bestseller? He wanted to, and he knew the perfect shop for it along the way. Like other perfectionists, however, he was somewhat fearful of being ridiculed—and now he worried about things going wrong in presenting her the flowers. He envisioned a few scenarios: for instance, the star of the event would be so swarmed by admirers that he wouldn't even be able to speak to her until it was all over, and would thus be left wandering around with the bouquet during the party, like an idiot. Instead, he arrived at the party empty-handed, and was less than happy with himself for doing so.

At the entrance to the banquet room were tall stacks of the new book, wreathed in arrangements of butterfly flowers (one of Karl Ástuson's favorite flowers, in fact). Hovering over these orange and purple tropical flowers was a cage holding two magnificent parrots, one deep red and the other bright blue. One of the parrots shrieked 'Bye-bye' over and over, in a mocking tone—which got on Karl Ástuson's nerves. When its 'Bye-bye' dwindled into 'Ai, ai,' the parrot's cage-mate took over and whistled the opening bars of the French national anthem, out of tune. A crowd had gathered around the man with no flowers, trapping him inconveniently close to the noises from the tuneless parrot. But the secret name for Doreen Ash's book had been revealed: *The Good Lover.*

Clever title. Excellent, in fact. Hard to believe it had never occurred to anyone before. But it wasn't really convincing for a supposed scientific textbook. He couldn't control himself, plucked a copy out from under the butterfly flowers and scrutinized it. The blurb on the back cover stated that the book's author had invented a new literary genre: a reality novel with a theoretical twist. A reality novel with a theoretical twist?? A romance novel. He opened the book, which was dedicated to Liina Minuti, with thanks for her invaluable assistance.

Karl Ástuson fumbled nervously while putting the copy back in its place, damaging part of a butterfly flower at the same time. An elderly couple with an academic air caught him in the act and gave him slightly indignant looks.

This was not a good start. He would rather not make any more blunders today and remained awkwardly in the back of the room—as far as he could from the crowd surrounding the best-selling author-to-be. He stared at the huge portraits of the brightly smiling Doreen Ash hanging over the podium, flanked by pictures of the book's cover. Doreen Ash had nicely shaped teeth. The cover was impressive. An orange and violet butterfly flower, painted over a black-and-white photo of two hands, a little one and a big one. A child's hand and an adult's hand. Not such a bad idea for a work that was supposed to be a mix of fiction and scholarship.

Karl Ástuson munched down some excellent canapés and polished off a glass of red wine at record speed. He wanted to get out of there, but first he had to congratulate the author and have her sign a copy of the book for him, as Doreen Ash had mentioned. Anything else would be cowardly. A betrayal. It would matter to her, at this important hour, to see him, even briefly. If what she told him the day before yesterday was true.

He could hardly believe it, standing there at this publication party, that it could be true. That the star of the day was in love with him. This woman, who was so far removed from his own world—had still managed to nestle herself there, like an egg in an ectopic pregnancy.

The couple with the academic air were suddenly right next to him. The woman said: 'You look so familiar; did we meet somewhere recently?'

Karl Ástuson said that that might very well be. He just couldn't recall where, but there was no purpose in asking him because he wasn't good with faces. He focused his attention on the couple, and thus was completely unprepared when the star came sailing over: Doreen Ash, younger and more elegant then when they first met; Doreen Ash in a black dress with a flared, white lined collar and a black necklace, looking straight out of a movie—Ingrid Bergman in *Casablanca*? 'You look stunning,' said Karl Ástuson, after kissing Doreen Ash on the cheek.

'I've gotten some sleep since we met. Sleep is the key to one's appearance, and the only thing that has an immediate effect.'

Well, something other than sleep had played a part in creating her appearance—her face and hair being made up and styled immaculately. A look that verged on being over the top, but was, in the end, striking. And a striking bracelet of platinum and lapis lazuli—which, strictly speaking, didn't go with the black necklace.

Karl Ástuson was off-balance, literally, and was lucky to be standing next to a table on which he could steady himself, discreetly. And the table became no less handy when Doreen Ash took a copy of *The Good Lover* from her purse and handed it to him.

'Thank you,' he said. 'I would really appreciate it if you would sign it for me.'

'I already have,' she said.

127

'Oh, thank you,' he said, but hesitated to open the book to see what she had written.

'And thank you for engraving your name on the bracelet,' she said.

'You're welcome. I hope it won't cause any trouble at home.'

'I haven't really been waving it in front of Liina. Anyway, she has a philosophical attitude.'

'Oh, I thought you said she was jealous.'

'She is. But she's not making my life difficult with bullshit. I wouldn't live with her if she did. You can't live with people who are always giving you shit.'

'Is she here?' asked Karl Ástuson.

'Yes,' said Doreen Ash, and she pointed at a small, dark-haired woman in a black dress suit and white shirt. She stood amid a crowd of people, talking and gesticulating.

'She's telling them what a great book this is,' said Doreen Ash. 'Of course she would say that; she put so much into it.'

'I look forward to reading it,' said Karl.

'That you should definitely do,' said Doreen Ash.

'A combination of a novel and textbook?'

'It's not so far removed to call it a reality novel with a theoretical twist, as it says on the cover.'

'Sounds exciting,' said Karl Ástuson.

'Yes, at least I thought so while I was writing it,' said Doreen.

'I've never heard of a reality novel with a theoretical twist.'

'I'm not surprised. I invented the genre.'

'So you're doing something brand new.'

'New in the way that I've done it, as far as I know. But there's really nothing new under the sun. At most, under localized sunbeams.'

'How long did it take you?' asked Karl, who felt more comfortable in more down-to-earth conversations.

'Two years—I finished it about a year ago.'

'I'm sure it's going to do extremely well,' said Karl.

A tall man approached and signaled Doreen that it was time to move along.

She introduced them: 'My publisher, Jasper Masters; my friend Carl Astason.'

'I guess I've got to go say a few words,' she said. 'Don't leave without saying goodbye.'

'I won't,' said Karl, laying his hand on her arm. She looked at his hand, and then looked him in the face and smiled. He saw in her smile that they would not meet again, not after this occasion; that she had decided that that was best—and he watched her walk away and engraved her in his memory, as she made her way across the room to ascend the podium. She had a dignified and deliberate air.

Doreen Ash began speaking, and she was brilliant. An American star. She had a polished, somewhat academic style. She was entertaining. She did not try to capture attention with cheap tricks and gestures, but instead, kept things light and composed. She spoke the most beautiful English, without any particularly distinguishable accent. Her voice and articulation were clear and fluid. Her mannerism at the podium was impeccable—which was more than could be said about her mannerism in other situations. Who was this person? And what had she actually written?

The way she described the book, it could be an incredible experiment. Definitely that, and maybe more. A romance written by a psychiatrist, in which both parties are scrutinized and analyzed scientifically. In other words, what she did was treat the lovers as a kind of case study, while describing in detail what went on between them, one afternoon, and one evening as it progressed into night—so minutely that she called it 'reality fiction.'

Karl Ástuson's mind wandered during her speech. He

doubted whether this could be good literature. A romance framed by professional clichés, watered down with professional clichés or skewered by them. Was this not a case of two incompatible worlds in one book? Clever to come up with the idea, though. The woman had an acute intellect—that mustn't be forgotten. Who knows, maybe she had actually managed to get away with this presumptuous undertaking; had created something great from this unseemly mishmash.

He suddenly realized that Liina Minuti was sizing him up. Something about it reminded him unavoidably of the time when Doreen put on her glasses in bed and studied him. He decided to smile at her. Liina smiled back, rather sternly. She had a serious demeanor, and clear-cut facial lines. It was obvious from a distance that she wore no make-up. A pretty woman, but unintriguing.

At this point in the author's speech, both parrots went into overdrive at the same time, spitting out a cheeky string of 'Bye-byes' that carried loud and clear into the banquet room.

'They can't wait to read *The Good Lover*,' said Doreen Ash, prompting laughter from the throng of guests. Liina Minuti rushed to the door and shut it.

Doreen Ash concluded her speech with style and the room applauded her enthusiastically. First her publisher kissed her—and then kisses came from all sides and the applause continued until the publisher spoke up and asked for everyone's attention.

The publisher was a handsome man who did not look any less like a movie star than the author. What he said about *The Good Lover* and its author made Karl Ástuson feel as proud as if he himself had a share in the book. He caught himself smiling from ear to ear—until he noticed Liina Minuti's watchful eye.

In short, Doreen Ash had created a new literary genre, a

romance in which the lovers and their emotions are analyzed professionally over the course of the story. Supported, not least, by the author's independent theories, although the master, Sigmund Freud, was never distant—nor was the shadow of Melanie Klein. Without them, this book would not have been written, nor without the author's partner, the psychologist Liina Minuti, who had provided invaluable support. The publisher predicted great success for the book, and had had it printed in a large impression. He concluded his speech by saying that the basic undertone of the book was gravely serious, concerning the potential for love, the potential for individuals to live in love and with love. But the book was also written by a fantastic humorist, and humor added numerous dimensions to the work, which was multi-dimensional to begin with—and unique.

A wave of happy applause and laughter spread through the room. Jasper Masters, publisher, and Doreen Ash, author, shared a protracted hug.

The parrots went into overdrive once more; now siren whistles and caws of joy could be heard through closed doors.

Liina Minuti, brimming with love and admiration, was now in Doreen Ash's arms in place of the publisher. Karl Ástuson inched closer to them. He was curious to see them at close range. Liina was whispering something to Doreen. Karl felt for her. The person who was loved less, or almost not at all, was in a bad place. The person who gave everything and received crumbs in return—and certainly not the one thing she or he desired most, the love of her dearly beloved, his dearly beloved. Yet wasn't it better to be able to be with the one you loved, no matter how strict the limitations? Yes, how many unhappy lovers, men and women, have asked themselves that same question?

Doreen Ash freed herself from the long embrace, looked at

Karl as if no one else was in the room, and walked over to him.

'I'm so happy you came,' she said.

'I'm happy I was able to come. I won't forget this moment anytime soon. Thank you for inviting me, and good luck.'

'Thanks.'

'I'm so excited that I haven't even dared to open the book and have a look at your inscription.'

'I understand,' said Doreen Ash. 'Goodbye.'

'Goodbye,' said he.

'I wish you every happiness,' she said.

'I have it. I wouldn't have had it without you.'

'It warms my heart.'

She kissed him on the cheek and whispered: 'You're beautiful.'

'So are you,' he said. 'Never as much as today.'

'Never as much as today,' she repeated, and smiled as if she'd just had a clever idea that she wasn't going to share. Then she turned to a row of admirers.

Karl Ástuson left straightaway, with *The Good Lover* under his arm. He feared ending up in a conversation in which an explanation would be demanded as to why he had clear access to the star of the day. He didn't even risk waiting for the elevator, but took the stairs down, leaving the noisy attacks of the parrots behind. One of them said something that sounded like 'Shut your mouth,' in Danish.

While walking down nine floors, Karl Ástuson had the strange sensation that the book Doreen had given him was growing warmer in his hands, as a stone would: a beach pebble that he held in his palm on his walks with Ástamama and Una by the sea, out near Grótta, at Örfirisey.

Despite longing to get home to Long Island, to Una who drew him to her, constantly, his curiosity about the book grew stronger as it continued to grow warmer in his hand, as if it were made of an entirely different material than paper. Now he couldn't wait any longer to have a look inside. Involuntarily, he quickened his pace and headed to Grand Central Station. There, at an Italian restaurant upstairs, he was going to open the book.

Finally, he began to run. It was only after sitting down that he realized he'd run quite a stretch—he was drenched with sweat and panting. Karl Ástuson, fearful of ridicule, was glad that for the time being, he was the only guest at the restaurant. Luckily, the waiter was busy with something for the moment, and did not have a chance to throw him a disapproving look.

As he slowly caught his breath, he felt like a newcomer to the train stations of the world. He hardly recognized where he was or the atmosphere in general. Buzzing voices and shrill announcements, and down below him, flocks of people streaming every which way.

And on the table before him lay the book, *The Good Lover*, still unopened. He stared at the cover with its child's hand, adult hand, and butterfly flower, and momentarily considered throwing it away. This book would distract him. And he was in no hurry to have more distractions at the hands of Doreen Ash.

He had meant to order coffee and a Fernet Branca, because he was planning to have dinner with his dear Una, of course— yet when it came to it, he didn't ask for coffee and Fernet, but a veal steak and Chianti. The same thing he'd had that night with Doreen Ash, before they went to his place. If he'd been asked, he would have said that he was doing it for her, eating the same food. Since that night with him had changed so much for her, he was going to show her and that evening some solidarity and remember the goodness and fun that they'd shared. Including veal and Chianti. Do some justice to the memory. Wasn't it time to cross out the embarrassing part, with the smoking, etc.?

He hadn't yet opened *The Good Lover*, even though he could barely contain his curiosity. He waited for the waiter to bring the wine, had a sip straightaway (a real Chianti, luckily), took a deep breath and opened the book.

Written on the title page, in black ink, were the words:

For The Good Lover, himself.
With maximum love and gratitude,
Doreen Ash

Why associate love with maximum? The word that was associated with the prayer about sins and guilt: *Mea culpa, mea maxima culpa!* The prayer that he translated in his own way, and sometimes said to himself: 'My fault, entirely my fault!'

What sort of inscription was that: *For The Good Lover, himself*?

He closed the book hastily, went to the bathroom and splashed cold water on his face. What was that inscription? A little joke, in memory of one evening and one night three years ago? It had to be a joke, and he smiled at himself in the mirror and dried his face with his nicely pressed handkerchief.

His dinner was served. It was out of the question for him to bring his signed copy home. He had no other option but to throw it away. If he really wanted to, he could buy himself a clean copy. Or what?

It would probably be best if he didn't read this book. With an excessively personal inscription that amounted to a tasteless joke. He could probably get away with not reading it, because he would never have to discuss its contents with the author. Doreen Ash said as much with the look in her eyes: We won't see each other again. That was clear. Doreen Ash had a way of speaking clearly, not just with words. The effect was odd; both pleasant and unpleasant. Like an alternately hot and cold shower. It provided more robust circulation and well-being, but was unpleasant while it lasted.

Karl Ástuson looked up from his Italian veal, which he had begun to eat with gusto, and watched the lines of people hurrying in all directions with suitcases on wheels, backpacks, plastic bags, in a pattern that resembled rows of retreating ants. Where were all these people going, and what was in all those bags? Underwear, socks, shirts, books, toothbrushes.

Seventeen years ago he sat at Grand Central Station, having just arrived in the city, overwhelmed by its size and power, overwhelmed at the majesty and chaos of the train station, overwhelmed at being alone in the big world and all alone in his small one. No Ástamama to call and say: 'I'm in New York, where I said I was going.' No Una to hug. And he, the birthday boy, wept as he sat there on a step to regain strength for the last stage of his trip.

Many years later, he learned of the book *By Grand Central Station I Sat Down and Wept*. One of his lovers had quoted this title when he confided in her about his journey, the start of his stay in America, the tears. It was an absolute exception for him to confide in a lover about anything that mattered, and it was against the rules, which he had named Work Rules, just to poke fun at himself. He'd been so upset about this violation of his own rules that he forgot the name of this lover. Generally, he honored these women by remembering their names.

He stared at his food and the glass of wine and the copy of *The Good Lover* and listened closely to the announcements coming over the loudspeaker, as verification that he was in Grand Central Station, seventeen years later, and that Una, eternally lost, had come all the way to him.

He had envisioned the life ahead of him as he sat there on the steps and wept. He would live in America, he would become wealthy, he would have lovely homes in wonderful places, he was going to travel far, live in luxury, and have numerous lovers. The only thing that mattered, Una regained, he could not envision for the life of him. But in a distant, poorly lit recess of his soul, he had hoped so fervently for Una that he put everything he had into being worthy of her. Buying houses that she would adore. Furniture to her liking. China and cutlery. And she said, in both places: 'It's as if I chose these myself.'

And he answered, in both places: 'You did.'

He still hadn't looked through the book. Why not? Was he afraid of a book, or what? What sort of wimpiness was this? He stopped eating, pushed his plate away, opened the book and looked over the table of contents, where, among other things, he found these chapter titles: *In the Beginning was the Sun ... The Night as it Happened ... Narcissus without a Father ... Mirror of the Mother's Eye ... The Half-Sister Complex ... Love Mother ...*

He flipped through a few more pages before reading, starting from the beginning: Chapter One: *In the Beginning was the Sun.*

She was hurrying to meet friends on Broadway when a spot of sunlight on the corner of 7th and 55th drew her in. It was an occasion for champagne when the tough old sun managed to squeeze between skyscrapers and land on the sidewalk outside the bar and the luggage store. It was the sort of spring day when promises are made of more spring with a long summer in its wake, when it's easy to let oneself be carried off course, stand inadvertently out on the sidewalk and become one with the city: the incipient glory of the leaves in Central Park, the vigorous joggers and noisy birds. On one such afternoon in the capital of the world, great things were brewing.

So the dear woman had pilfered the bar and the sidewalk outside the luggage store. Maybe it wasn't unusual for a novelist to use locales he'd visited, rather than unfamiliar ones.

He himself was just coming out of the Apple store and was on his way to his usual restaurant on the next street, the Italian one. But he too was carried off course and wandered inadvertently toward the sun, and there he came across a woman in a white wrap dress standing alone on the sidewalk beneath a scaffolding, drinking champagne. Not really his type; he noticed immediately. Strictly speaking, not pretty enough, and on the older side. But there was something about her and her dress in the sun (first-class legs, for sure) that caused him to go into the bar and order champagne. He just managed to catch her on the sidewalk as she finished her drink.

He: There's no way I'm staying inside now that the sun is finally out.
She: I've been chasing after the sun since I can remember.
He: Just as well it wasn't rainbows.

And she threw him a quick glance, as if these words moved her. (In the book, however, neither the particular expression she wore nor anything touching on it was mentioned.)

He continued reading: the description of the man who passed by, which was obviously a description of Karl Ástuson; that much was certain. His appearance and his demeanor described in detail. Same with his clothing. The white shirt, dark gray trousers, the bluish-gray sweater he carried on his arm.

She had remembered this clearly. Nothing missing there. He knew that the bluish-gray sweater was correct, because he'd bought it that same day. But didn't it reveal a tangible lack of imagination that she should repeat in precisely the same words what they had said to each other? It was true—the introduction had been so perfect in its own way, in that sunny spot by a green suitcase at the start of spring—in that respect, it was impossible to improve—but wasn't the role of an author to add something new to reality? Reality itself was not one damned bit fiction, and could never be so. Reality was reality, and fiction fiction. Fiction was supposed to be truer than reality, which is why reality fiction, as Doreen Ash called it, had to be an even bigger lie than what really happened. Or were these words, lie and truth, irrelevant in this case?

It would never have occurred to him to take what she had written personally. She had obviously meant to use him as a prop. The material for the book, the content, she had to have derived from somewhere else. They hadn't been in a relationship; they were strangers to each other, and still were to this day. One night, and the rest happened in Doreen Ash's head. She would hardly have written about that. Reality fiction, she'd said—but there was so little actual reality to work with. One evening and half a night. That could hardly be enough for a thick book, even if their evening had started early. She could hardly spin out the story endlessly according to some fantasy she had in her head. One-sided love, and imagination. What kind of plot would that be? A pretty thin one.

Karl Ástuson continued to read about the conversation on the sidewalk in its detailed retelling. Until they moved inside to escape the spring breeze, which they found a bit too chilly. They took seats beneath a picture of Ronald Reagan and ordered another glass of champagne. And an old woman at the next table gave them the eye. She was wearing a white baseball cap and drinking a white, frothy drink through a straw. All correct.

He read on, but found it unexciting. He remembered the evening quite well and could have written such a retelling himself, if it came down to it. It was obvious that he wasn't reading a book by a real novelist. It was hard to tell whether other readers might find the narrative worth their while—but for him it was flavorless, because he knew it by heart.

How was this imaginatively challenged author going to continue, when it turned out that she couldn't even make good use of the sparse material that their evening and night had provided, and which wasn't enough for a book, even if it were stretched and pulled with something called a theoretical twist? It would be interesting to see how she went about it, when it was obvious that a direct description of the undramatic events of the evening wouldn't cover it. He checked again; yes, it was 570 pages. A ghastly habit, and very much in the American style, to spin out such gigantic tomes.

Karl Ástuson cut his veal, which had cooled off, into smaller bites, before attacking it with the fork in his right hand, as he held the open book in his left and read like every other reader out there—until Doreen Ash began to describe what happened next, with the wisdom of hindsight. Then he abruptly put his fork down and took the book in both hands.

She saw in hindsight when she fell for the man—the precise moment when he slipped into her consciousness in such a way that there was no turning back; a man whom she would love from that moment on without being able to help it.

It was when he smiled, after having said: *Just as well it wasn't rainbows*—when she saw the beginning of the smile; how his face moved with the smile, from his eyes to his mouth; how the seriousness of a man walking by with a sweater on his arm transformed into the lightness of the man on the sidewalk with a glass of champagne, how incredibly sweet and boyish his smile was. An unconditional smile.

Most smiles are conditional, said this writer. Which is lovely ... BUT so many things can be even lovelier, when it comes down to it. And above all, don't come too near that smile.

But here was a smile that was nothing but what it was, the smile itself, like the prototype for all others, like the forerunner of the very first smile in the world. You fall for such a smile unconditionally, immediately; it was right, it was certain; there was no avoiding it.

Yet even if you fell for it immediately and unconditionally, you didn't realize it as it happened, not fully. Because that was the nature of time and life, and all that mattered most in life. It didn't become clear until later how much it mattered. In this case, half a day had passed since the event, since the smile, before she realized. It was love. Inescapable. Irrevocable.

It wasn't just that she knew exactly what she had fallen for; she also knew the precise time. She happened to be on her way to meet friends of hers on Broadway, so she glanced at her watch before stepping into the bar on the corner and asking for champagne.

How unsuspecting she'd been about what was to happen over the next few minutes: meeting a man who would change everything and leave her head over heels in love and abandoned on the paths of emptiness, from that point on.

For the second time in his life, Karl Ástuson sat in Grand Central Station and wept. He wept for himself as he sat on those steps on his twentieth birthday, with all he owned in his hands: a suitcase of belongings, and emptiness. He wept about how close he had come to having Doreen's emptiness follow him the rest of his life. He wept about his life from the moment it ended, when Una left him on the Tuesday morning following Merchants' Weekend, until it began again, seventeen-and-a-half years later, on a February night when she came walking up the steps at Silfurströnd 5, in a long purple woolen coat. He wept for Doreen Ash and the story of love that was consistent with what she herself had told him in her office. He wept for the woman who was then condemned to live life as he had done all those years, in a loveless void, because it was loveless despite Liina loving her; lovelessness is not being loved by those you love.

There was nothing else to do but close the book, which was, unfortunately, about him, *himself*, and ask for the check. The waiter came right away with the bill and an extra napkin, so that his customer could dry his eyes and blow his nose. (His nicely pressed handkerchief was fully used.) No one but this waiter, who had greeted him with an exaggerated Italian bow, had noticed the weeping man in Grand Central. Every day someone weeps somewhere in Grand Central Station; it is one of the best places in the world for weeping. Not just in a book. In the misty fog of his tears, Karl Ástuson debated whether he should throw away *The Good Lover* and go home to Una on Long Island, or continue reading on the New York side. He could not go home with this copy. Wouldn't it be best to toss it into a well-chosen trash can, and be rid of it for good? This book was in his way. It was a lion in his path. An unexpected distraction. It could even do him great harm, maybe. But only if he continued reading it. Should he risk it? The privileged man who had started life number two with the girl of his dreams—because that was what she was, Una, his storybook princess, his only love, the stuff of his dreams, day in and day out, through the years. No book was allowed to skew the golden ratio of his and Una's new life. It was his task to stave off all distractions, no matter how, deal with them swiftly and securely once and for all, minimize the effects of the damage. In order to be able to continue undaunted and undistracted, with the precious life that he'd been granted anew, against all odds.

It was too much of an effort to break away from Grand Central Station. He was on his way out with the book in his hand when he noticed a step and sat down on it—just as he had done after arriving in the city. His tears were gone, but he was still consumed with sadness, without understanding precisely where it came from, to the man who had Una on Long Island, Una who would soon be cuddling under an Icelandic eiderdown duvet and waiting for him to come to her.

He opened the book and reread the inscription, which transformed him into a storybook hero, a role model, written in the author's determined, yet delicate hand. Every letter clearly defined. No mistaking any of it.

 He continued to read where he had left off. The description of what passed between him and Doreen continued, in detail—how they sat and stood. Incredible how accurately she described reality—that she should barely ever stray from a single thing in order to spice up reality, round it off. The outcome was accordingly square.

The hero, Karl Ástuson, was blocking the path of a man on his way down the stairs with a big suitcase, and was lucky the man didn't tumble over him. He closed the book, stood up, and forced himself out onto the street. He wandered aimlessly down the broad and busy avenues, incapable of throwing away the signed book and going home, as he would have preferred to do. He ended up checking himself into the nearest hotel so that he could continue his reading undistracted. It was a colorless, three-star hotel with a nondescript lobby.

It was very unlike him to stay at anything but a proper hotel, but this was an emergency; he had no time to look for anything better. The time that he had to read *The Good Lover* was slipping away; he couldn't be staying out late into the evening without letting Una know his whereabouts. This was a book that he would not be able to open again after tonight; it was a threat to Una and himself.

If he were still living his former life, the book wouldn't have mattered. He probably would have thought it and the whole situation funny, if he hadn't happened to have gone all-in in an attempt to rebuild his life in a way very few people ever get a chance to do. Now he faced the difficult task of dealing with the fanatical intervention of a force of destiny whose role ought to have been finished, and he had to be tough and focused.

He desperately wanted to take a shower, but there was no time. He would have preferred to stay the night, but he couldn't lie to Una, and besides, he would have found it very difficult to come up with a lie. The last thing he wanted to do was make her feel suspicious of anything. Suspicious of an affair. What a silly word that was: 'affair!' He was grateful only to know of it from hearsay—that he'd never been in a position to cheat; that he would forever be spared the fate of being a cheater.

Karl Ástuson, who wanted nothing more than to take a shower, took off his shoes, sat with his legs stretched before him on the hotel bed with its beige cover, arranged the pillows, made himself comfortable, and opened the book about himself. He looked around before starting to turn the pages, and it was as he had expected: a horribly ugly hotel room. Everything in it was tasteless. He found himself facing a print of *The Scream* by Munch. Was he in Oslo, or New York? He didn't want that image facing him here and now. He got out of bed and turned *The Scream* toward the wall.

He wasn't able to make himself comfortable again. Extremely irritated, he began trying to find his counterpart in the novel. What on earth would she name him? He found it on page 53, when they were sitting down to dine at the restaurant *Mamma Mia!* His name was Carl Söhnlein, an American man who had a Swedish mother. Good thing he wasn't the Icelander Karl Ástuson. How would he have explained THAT to Una if she made the mistake of reading this book? On the other hand, he was really not happy with the name Söhnlein—which he thought might mean 'Sonny.' And besides, it was the name of a cheap German sparkling wine. Something about this combination of bubbles and a little boy rubbed Karl Ástuson the wrong way, and he cursed the book's author, Doreen Ash, under his breath.

A Swedish mother, yes—but what about the father? Who was his father supposed to be, and what nationality? She wouldn't dare give her protagonist an undetermined paternity, would she?

Karl Ástuson flipped through the pages agitatedly but found no mention of his counterpart's paternity; only much more about his eyes—oh that green luster, yes, oh oh! She wasn't particularly successful with such descriptions. Clichés about inner glow and the sea. Quite clearly, the author had no grasp of the craft of fiction. And her scholarship was careless. Would her colleagues be amused?

The reader in the hotel room had flipped quickly through half of the book. The accurate descriptions continued, to his horror, and there was a growing seriousness in the analyses of the characters' personalities, their behavior, what went on between them. Not everything was favorable to The Good Lover, oh no—no matter what high marks he got for his behavior, caresses, his voice, his looks. The author, for instance, portrayed him as incapable of giving, except when it came to lovemaking, when he'd given his all—while imagining another woman.

This lack of generosity had, in other respects, reared its head in the way, among other things, that he very cleverly and skillfully diverted conversations away from himself, whenever the author broached a subject of any importance. A predetermined game, a tried-and-tested plot; everything was channeled toward one brief encounter, which wasn't meant to leave anything special behind, other than the memory of a beautiful façade, a smooth and polished interaction, once, just for fun.

The author continued on her insolent course by giving detailed examples from real life of how The Good Lover went about avoiding important questions, how he went about immediately cutting threads that could have lead in his direction—how determined he had been never to make any indication that they would ever meet again. You had to hand it to the author, though—for her part, she found this an honest approach.

The reader still hadn't found anything in connection with the key issue of paternity, but there were entire half pages about his hands, artistically alluring fingers that did everything right, whether it was holding a fork and knife or touching anything momentarily, for instance the back of the author's hand. He had now run through a number of paragraphs about his own hands, and was beginning to feel more than anxious about how the author would treat these fingers once they were in bed together. She was likely to recount everything in intimate detail. Was he really supposed to read all that, too? Wasn't it time to stop and destroy The Good Lover once and for all?

Why continue with such painful reminiscences, now that the 'Good-Lover chapter' in his life was finished? The lover of lovers no longer existed. He was the lover of one woman. A one-woman lover. How bloody INTOLERABLE it was that Doreen Ash had decided to raise a monument to his former life, that empty and trivial life, which he might just as well have done without, yes, literally done without, and just killed himself—except that he was then laying the foundation for his storybook future with Una. Without knowing it—but definitely heading toward that goal. Working hard to become rich and richer. Creating the paradise in the south of France for Una. Decorating the house on Long Island to suit Una's taste, in her colors—where it had been waiting, ready for her, for eight years. And this subconscious, long-term plan that had been a success, against all odds—had now suffered a serious setback. A sending?

There was no small amount of resentment and vindictiveness in that sending (despite the love). No small amount of bitterness mixed with the sweetness. Karl Ástuson considered himself a step ahead of the highly-learned author when it came to some of the analytical details. It was very questionable whether Doreen Ash was aware that some of what she had written was extremely embarrassing for The Good Lover— even what was supposedly well and beautifully meant.

And the paternity? It finally came to him to look for it at the same point when he had revealed his paternity in real life, or rather, his lack of it—when Doreen Ash was about to walk out the door of his house. He hastily skipped over their lovemaking, with all the extras; he flipped through their conversation on the couch, and came to where she was about to walk out the door—and sure enough, there it was.

Carl Söhnlein's paternity was undetermined. (Fucking bitch!)

A purebred motherson. A Narcissus who did not gaze at his own reflection in a pool in the woods, like the original one, but instead, in his mother's eyes—and he had those eyes all to himself; there was no competition for that mirror, nor for the mother's breast. Here was a Narcissus and suckler of all times, who not only sat alone at the mirror of his mother's eyes, but also sat alone at his mother's breast. After leaving these, he searched for a mother—even more intensely and passionately than a normal man, despite a normal man's search for a mother being extensive and deep enough already. In an attempt at humor, the author wrote: *The main thing here is not having a woman in every port, but rather, a mother in every woman.*

The author, Doreen Ash, came to the conclusion that it was logical for a purebred motherson to excel as a lover, as Carl Söhnlein, of undetermined paternity, did. From a very early age, he'd been undistracted by any thought of rivalry with other men. He was completely at ease with himself at his mother's bosom, without the faintest idea who his father was, an idea that could have been a hindrance. He was eternally in love with one woman, his mother, and incapable of falling in love with any other women than her—and the key to his skill as a lover was his utter lack of affection for his targets, and unperturbed by distracting feelings of love when he was satisfying a woman.

Here followed a long, theoretical treatise on mothersons, peppered with quotations from articles by the author and other scholars. The basis for the treatise was the Freudian idea that the first and perhaps only object of a man's love is his mother.

Next, the author, in an extremely detailed, verbose style that Karl Ástuson felt had little place in a literary text (and perhaps it was not supposed to be one, after all), harped on about her notion that the most purebred type of motherson was the one with an undetermined paternity—he who did not know who his own father was. And then came her knock-out punch. Mothersons of all times and Jesus Christ were shown to be comparable in general, and the motherson of undetermined paternity and Jesus Christ in particular; they were one and the same type, because naturally, Jesus Christ had an uncertain paternity—had no idea who his real father was. A paternity that was such a great secret that he became the son of a mother who had to be a virgin even though conception had taken place, yes, a virgin after giving birth—all this to cover up the dubious and erotic relationship between mother and son, how a mother compensates for her disappointment in love and a bad husband (what was the poor carpenter, Joseph, to do?) by making her sonny boy an eternal cutie pie and surrogate lover. Here Doreen Ash cited the short story 'Judas,' by Frank O'Connor, in which the mother competes directly with the girlfriend, and finally emerges victorious, clutching her sobbing son to herself with the logical, endearing words: 'My little man.'

Carl Söhnlein, alias Karl Ástuson, jumped out of bed and flung *The Good Lover* violently into a corner. He stared at the battered book lying there on the mold-brown carpet, then grabbed it and followed up on the former procedure by ripping out the inscribed page, tearing it into tiny pieces, tossing them into the toilet and flushing. The rest of the book, he would dispose of in a well-chosen trashcan on his way home. He wasn't going to buy another copy of this book, never open it beyond the walls of the spiritless dumpster that this hotel room was— an appropriate place to skim through a load of crap about oneself, which a desperate author had mashed together from a deep lack of knowledge of her subject matter, especially when it came to the emotional life of Karl Ástuson, the hero of the story.

Karl Ástuson looked at the book about Doreen Ash and Karl Ástuson. He looked at his shoes by the bed. What should he do, put on his shoes and head home, making a secretive stop at a trashcan, or take one last look inside the book? Of course he was curious to see how she would narrate their lovemaking. Would it be obscene? Sentimental? Would she describe everything precisely as it was, or would she finally allow herself some deviation? Use her imagination? No, how could she? She simply didn't have any. The whole book bore witness to a deplorable lack of imagination. Was this the extent of her ambition, to stick so ridiculously close to every detail of reality, to repeat it? That's what this book was. Nothing more than goddamn repetition. With some scholarly clichés that read more like excuses. The result was clear: Doreen Ash would be better off sticking to the sciences. She had picked up some speed on that rollercoaster.

Karl Ástuson sat down on the bed, his teeth clenched in frustration despite the feeling of curiosity still burning inside him. What kind of lover was he then, this Good one? Best to find out. He flipped through the pages until he came to their first kiss.

He touched my shoulder, and my soul was aroused.

How absurd. When he touched a lover's shoulder, it wasn't to touch her soul, but to touch her shoulder. He who'd been deprived of the only love in his life, and therewith life itself, had no other option but to grope in a roundabout way toward love and life, and no matter how distant love and life continued to be, he gained a sort of grounding by having a lover for a few hours. Wasn't he entitled to that, at least?

He touched my shoulder, and my soul was aroused.

He ordered himself to close this twisted book, but was too curious to obey. Particularly now that he'd caught a tiny glimpse of some talent on the part of the author. She'd stopped smothering the reader with clichés. The narration was sincere, and her confidence had risen. At the same time, the reader's fear increased. He read fast, as if the Devil were on his tail. Took care not to dwell on particulars, allowing as little as possible to sink in.

Karl Ástuson never understood how he managed to avoid being proud of himself and his performance in lovemaking. The book stated bluntly: The Good Lover was not just a good lover, he was a dream lover, what all women dreamed of. And what women dreamed of was expounded in detail. Finally, he knew.

With growing astonishment, he read the details of their lovemaking. At times, he couldn't really tell that this was the two of them, he and Doreen Ash, being described. The author had finally adopted the technique of leaving out significant details. Not a single letter was written here about how she had given her good lover instructions—verbally, and not particularly delicately; and not just once, but twice.

No, in her book, the two exchanged no words as they made love; no words were needed. Everything was perfect without words. The lover's extreme sensitivity and passion were given highest praise—at the same time as the suspicion was expressed that he was thinking of an entirely different woman. It shouldn't have been possible to pick up a woman on the street and bring her to such a climax without some emotional preparation.

Yes, and what a climax it was; the author found herself lost for words to describe it, and was forced to quote from *For Whom the Bell Tolls* by Ernest Hemingway, where an orgasm makes the earth move. Then there were some awkward comments about an epiphany, a religious experience.

Well. The dear woman hadn't really given him the impression of having had a supernatural experience when, at the conclusion of their amorous game, she stared at him through her spectacles and smoked—and even blew the smoke in his direction.

The author continued in the orgasm department, inching her way toward her main point: the fact that Carl Söhnlein didn't want to have an orgasm provided even better support for the theory that he had another woman in mind. The reader smirked at how the author failed to mention how she'd suggested coercing an orgasm out of him by hand when nothing else worked.

Now Doreen Ash turned away from the lovemaking. Ominous analyses were forthcoming. The fact that The Good Lover denied himself an orgasm was lumped together with the love of a purebred motherson for his mother—since the mother was in all women, and the incest must not be consummated with an orgasm; the risk of conceiving a child with one's mother.

This was the final straw for Karl Ástuson, protagonist and reader. He was going to deal with this book once and for all. Before he closed *The Good Lover* for the last time, however, he thought he would take just a little look at how Doreen Ash dealt with what followed their lovemaking; that is, the smoking in bed. Whether she was going to smoke her cursed cigarettes there in print, too. No, it didn't seem so, at a glance. Just as well for her to edit it out.

The reader stuck the book about himself in his jacket pocket and left the hotel room that was so completely beneath him that the receptionist tried to make himself invisible when he returned the key.

When he was met by the evening breeze, he recalled what he had said when Doreen Ash called him a purebred motherson: 'Material for a book, maybe?' That's what he had said. Could he have brought this upon himself?

The darkness in the city was no longer tepid. And Karl Ástuson was not dressed warmly enough against the cool darkness. It couldn't be helped; no one would have carried a sweater on his arm to a publication party under a blazing spring sun. It hadn't even been yesterday; it had been today, but he felt as if at least a week had gone by since he watched Doreen Ash give a speech in a black-and-white star dress, engulfed in admiration and love. Admiration that she deserved for being brilliant, and a good person in her own special way.

And that was apparently the best you could be: good in your own way—because kindness is the most specialized phenomenon of the soul. On the other hand, a good and intelligent person had made the mistake of writing a contemptible book. It was humiliating to take a man whom you had slept with once, only too willingly—and concoct an embarrassing text in which his emotional life is pseudo-scientifically analyzed on an atomic scale. To protect herself, or rather, to exalt herself. But such was life: even the most impressive of people, and that included Doreen Ash as well, yes, even they were small-minded when it came down to it. Blamed others and exalted themselves. Maybe there was no other possible way to exist—but to imagine deep inside that you're more important than others. In this, as he knew so well, it naturally helped for a man to have the best mom in the world.

When he emerged from the hotel, Karl Ástuson still felt aimless, so much so that he didn't take the train home to Long Island straightaway, but instead wandered over to the bar where he had found Doreen Ash. Because it had certainly been he who found her. The neon sign above the bar was broken; the letters that worked spelled ASH. A joke. Yet another one. He went in, sat down at the table beneath the picture of Ronald Reagan and asked for a glass of champagne.

At that moment, he missed Doreen Ash; he wanted to talk to her, hear her say something surprising and even something uncomfortable, in her husky voice. At the same time, he was terribly discontent with himself, for daring to miss another woman besides Una. He had let Una and himself down, and he felt sorry for himself. To have become so indelibly entangled in Doreen Ash's consciousness and to have had to pay the price for it by being seriously distracted from his own great strategy for happiness. He had become a man in a book, and a rather lousy copy, at that. Even if the author hadn't meant it that way. Not consciously.

The situation rankled him deeply: to be sitting beneath a picture of Ronald Reagan and missing Doreen Ash. He could not, however, have foreseen that he would be glad in retrospect to have missed her—for a reason that would come to light with the new day.

He stared into space, which slowly condensed into a fog. Vague outlines of chairs and tables and a few hazy guests. This illusion was enough to frighten any sane man, but he enjoyed it, if anything, and finished his champagne slowly.

When the haze cleared, the old lady from the next table over back in the day had taken a seat in her spot, still wearing a white baseball cap, still sipping on a frothy white drink through a straw—looking slightly younger than she did three years ago. Who was her doctor?

He nodded at the old lady as he passed by, and she nodded back, thoughtfully, as if she knew something he did not; and she probably did.

Now it was very dark on Doreen's sidewalk, because a light in the pole on the corner had died just as he stopped at the bar. He imagined the sunny spot by the green suitcase—it was three years ago—and the woman in the white wrap dress with the champagne glass, at a one-woman party, until he came and said:

There's no way I'm staying inside now that the sun is finally out.

It was a beautiful memory; he was going to keep it and throw away the rest, and that is what he did. *The Good Lover* ended up in a trashcan on the corner beneath the defective light pole, apart from the inscribed page that was now on a tattered journey through the sewage system of New York.

For The Good Lover, himself.
With maximum love and gratitude,
Doreen Ash

An inscription for a storybook hero, gone for eternity. The acquaintanceship between the author and the protagonist in the shredder of time, where it would be shredded in peace, if it were up to him. And of course it was up to him. There was no way that the author would make life hell for him. She would leave him be—especially since she had put the period at the end of his story. The Good Lover, as he had become, and then some. To forget all about him was another matter. According to all indications, she wouldn't do it; couldn't do it, not in this life.

When he arrived home, Una was asleep. She always slept on her side. He looked at her head resting on the pillow, how her short hair lay across her cheek, to the tip of her nose, like an upside-down fan. He looked at the cream-yellow strap on her nightdress, her slender shoulder and long upper arm, which he had known since he was eleven years old, and waited until she stirred. Then he touched her shoulder and said:

'I'm home. I'm sorry it took me so long.'

'That's all right, my love,' she said, and added: 'I've only just fallen asleep.'

He took a shower, and then relaxed on the sofa with a gin and tonic, his and Doreen's drink. At that, the circle was closed. The book as well; not just closed, but destroyed in two stages.

At his final sip, warm compassion snuck up on Karl Ástuson, and his frustration gave way. Coincidence had brought them together, him and one woman, and she couldn't forget him, was stuck with him, unmovable, like a two-hundred-kilogram body washed up on the beach. The son of Ástamama was feeling ashamed of himself for this unsavory comparison when the truth about love and facts dawned on him.

Who, if not he, should understand that love is a fact, that feelings are facts, probably the only thing in life that are facts, apart from the day you're born and the day you die. Memories, what a human being is made of, are the most unreliable things in the world. The definition of a human being is a forgetful species—so forgetful that it doesn't even know what it is that it remembers. What it remembers correctly are feelings: love, fear, jealousy, anger; thus, feelings should rightly be called the facts of life—and particularly love, because that is the one that matters most. Perhaps it's the only thing that counts on the day of reckoning. Perhaps the only thing that's asked about, if anything is asked at all.

Concerning the fickleness of love, Karl Ástuson of all people should have known that true love never budges; it lives an independent life, on its own, outside everything, above everything and everyone except itself. If it so happens that it budges, it does so on its own terms; whoever gets in its way has no control over it. The woman who had written the ridiculous book about him was his comrade in suffering, and he suddenly felt incomprehensibly fond of her. In fact, she touched his heart, plain and simple; yes, like a half-sister, for instance.

When he crawled into bed with Una, she vanished into thin air: Doreen Ash, who had distracted him, yet had become something of a half-sister. It was night and Doreen Ash had lain down to rest like other creatures of the forest. Nothing existed but he and Una. He laid his hand over the woman and protected her. In her sleep, she took his hand and laid it to her lips. He felt warm to the core. He was a happy man. As such, he fell asleep, and as such he woke. A happy man. If a book were to be written about him, a true story, a reality novel, its most fitting title would be *A Happy Man*.

It was approaching noon. Una had not yet stirred, even when a ray of sunlight found its way to her temple. He got out of bed and went to make coffee and toast. Una didn't feel like getting up; she wanted to doze a little longer. She had slept badly; had dreamed a bad dream. Karl had carefully drawn the curtain shut, so that her temple would be left in peace from that aggressive sunbeam—so that she could recover from her bad dream.

He drank his coffee in the living room and went to get some work done. Doreen Ash was tranquil in her fenced patch, ruminating with eyes closed. He had turned a raging bull into a docile cow, and scratched it in spirit behind its ears as he sat there at his alchemist's desk. After working for an hour, he offered Una coffee again, but she wanted to continue to linger in bed.

He still had moments when he couldn't believe his eyes when he was close to Una. Now he hesitated there for a moment, just to be sure that it was she herself, safe and sound, slumbering there in his big bed, and not just a tanned leg on top the duvet.

This well-formed leg was unreal enough for Karl Ástuson to begin searching for other evidence of Una's presence, and he opened her closet in the dressing room. There was no mistaking it; there hung her clothes, which they had fun buying in Saks and Barneys on several sprees: little black dresses, big silk panties, purple sweatshirts. By cunning means, he had managed to wake a dormant clothesaholic, and his greatest achievement was finding high-heeled shoes that the woman was comfortable wearing. The connoisseur Karl had exceeded the connoisseur Una in every department and come up with such an exquisite wardrobe for her that an entire legion of stylists could not have done better.

He shut the closet carefully, returned to the living room, and contemplated happiness. This was his last chance before happiness demanded an unforeseen tribute—this dissimulator, happiness, which hadn't suffered any damage from the most obvious direction—Ingi Bói. He had washed his hands of Una, as if he couldn't have cared less. When it comes down to it, one never really knows another person; as Una did not know her husband. She had predicted that he would do everything he could to make her life miserable. Even more so, that he would pose a palpable threat. When it came down to it, his vanity had the upper hand; he acted as if didn't matter to him one whit, and hurriedly snapped up a twenty-five-year-old soprano singer who looked like Uma Thurman and wore the same red-black nail polish that she did in *Pulp Fiction*.

Karl Ástuson had come to the conclusion that happiness equated to easiness. At least everything with Una had been so easy, after they had first made love in Beauséjour, that it was almost miraculous. The world around them and their daily distractions were of little consequence, whether they had to do with work or Una's divorce; they just needed some prioritizing.

Like him, Una was good at prioritizing. This could be seen, for instance, in how she hadn't wanted to tarnish the Beau-séjour-bliss by talking about the Tuesday morning following Merchants' Weekend; instead, she let it wait until their second day in America, with her eye still swollen. It made a great difference. Karl could focus on her invisible eye as he listened to what he'd never wanted to hear.

Yes, she went camping in Þórsmörk with three friends: Lóa, Þórdís, and Helga. It was evening, Lóa was drunk, and peppered her with questions about her boyfriend. Her girlfriends listened. When Una told how she and Karl occasionally cooked fish and potatoes at his house in the evenings, Lóa burst into mean-spirited laughter. Then they all howled with laughter. All but Una. She said that there was nothing strange about them cooking together; he'd just lost his mom.

'Are you going to open an orphanage?' asked Lóa.

This really made Una's temper flare, and she retorted that Lóa was jealous because Karl was the cutest and funnest and best boy in all of Reykjavík, and she just had a crush on him herself.

In her anger and frustration, Una left the others and ended up in a tent with strangers and downed Icelandic schnapps straight from the bottle, which was something she'd never done before. She was feeling nauseous when one of the tent's occupants tried to kiss her and almost succeeded, but luckily, she had to vomit, and fell asleep afterward.

She woke up that Monday morning cold and wet (rain had leaked into the tent), and feeling terribly bent out of shape. She got a ride to town without talking to her friends, and realized that she wasn't good enough for Karl. A strange boy had kissed her. It was gross, and she'd thrown up.

'Was that it?' asked the man who'd been deprived of his love for seventeen years for no reason.

'Yes.'

'I can't believe it,' said Karl, still focusing on Una's swollen eye.

'And why didn't you ask me anything?' said Una, disheartened.

'I thought upright men didn't ask about anything when they were dumped. Are you saying that would have changed something?'

'If you had asked me and found out how silly it was and tried to comfort me, than maybe we would have been together this whole time.'

'You might have thought it more than just silly back then.'

'I can't believe I would have.'

They had to resign themselves to this fact, these exorbitantly happy people: that stuff and nonsense can be the cause of pro-longed destinies and shape entire lifetimes. Nothing else to do but to shake one's head and try to forget.

Yet Karl would not forget Lóa's part in this matter, and he wasn't a bit happy about her still being one of Una's friends. She was planning on coming and visiting sometime, but Karl put his foot down and said that there was no way she was wel-come to stay with them. He said he had a bad memory of her coming onto him quite vulgarly shortly after Una broke up with him.

Una laughed at this, and said that that had been in their former life. Karl looked at the woman, and envied her easygoing attitude. If he had had a friend who behaved like Lóa, their friendship would have been finished. Even if it had been a long time ago. He would never have spoken a word to him again.

He found Una's easygoing attitude exemplary, as well as her life's philosophy about worries: You can't prepare yourself for disaster by worrying. Worries are always useless and are nothing but trouble, because in the end, the disasters come from an entirely different direction than the obvious one—as was proven with Ingi B., for example.

When it came to material for concern, Karl had found time in the middle of their Beauséjour bliss to have doubts about Una in America. He was going to transplant her as if it were the simplest thing in the world; settle her there as if it were nothing; a person who had never been to that part of the world. (He even caught himself wondering how it was even possible never to have visited America.)

He would never have thought that Una, who had a critical mind (negative, on an Icelandic scale) would react to the new continent like a child in Disneyland. Everything reminded her of toys; red trucks with silver exhaust pipes, houses like enlarged versions of Fisher-Price toys. She also used the word 'cute' for the food in America. Everything drowned in sauces and melted cheese. Not exactly her style, but in her extraordinary tolerance, she said: 'Why not give it a try?'

It took Una twenty-four hours to make up her mind about making their home together in the new world. On their second day, they went for a drive around the Long Island neighborhood and took a walk on the beach by the house.

'I'd like to live here forever,' she said, and added unabashedly that Long Island was the only place she could picture living in America.

Karl, utterly amazed, said nothing, until it crossed his mind to tell her that by lucky coincidence, the house was in fact there. And followed up by asking why she had such a high opinion of Long Island. She responded by asking why he'd bought a house precisely there, and put so much effort into decorating it that he obviously wasn't going to camp out there just for one night. 'Well,' he said, 'it's because Long Island is an island of rustic bliss and beaches, right at the doorstep of New York City itself.'

'What did I tell you?' Una then said. 'There's no place like it in all the world.'

'The world's a big place,' said Karl, who'd seen a much larger chunk of it than Una.

'Let's go and see it,' said Una, and Karl promised to take her traveling. To places with golden beaches and a thousand green hills—where it takes an entire day and night to fly there and be reborn, as he had apparently done, naked in rain and sun, with a chattering parrot at his feet.

In retrospect, Karl Ástuson could not understand how he had sat himself down on the sofa in the middle of a workday, and even switched on the television. The man who generally didn't sit down on the sofa until the workday was finished, let alone watch television in the middle of the day.

He flipped from one channel to the next; there was a flood here and an eruption there. A man murdered in Brooklyn. And a newly published novelist, Doreen Ash, a psychiatrist, had died in Manhattan that morning. She had taken her own life. Her first novel, *The Good Lover*, had been published yesterday, and had been predicted to be a great success. The reviews that had already been published about it, however, were mixed: everything from high-flown praise to the harshest criticism. The book's author was forty-one years old.

Karl Ástuson turned off the T V and finished his coffee. He went into the music room, straight to the closet where he kept the old suitcase, the suitcase that he had brought with him to New York seventeen years ago. From it he took a lavender colored sweater that would fit a one-year-old. It had been in that suitcase from the start, and hadn't left it apart from the few times that he'd held it. He had done so the first night that Una spent with him on Long Island, when he couldn't sleep. He had gone to the music room, sat there with the sweater in his lap and thanked it for his newfound happiness. It was the sweater from Ástamama, the one she'd knitted the last weeks of her life, for the little girl she'd conveyed her greetings to when the time came.

Karl Ástuson hugged the sweater close before putting it back in its place and donning a tracksuit. He let Una know that he was going out for an hour or so, and that there was coffee in the coffeepot.

As soon as he stepped onto the sidewalk, he looked at his watch. He was going to run for precisely one hour—run away from Doreen Ash. Be done with her, as far as that were possible. A woman had died. Doreen Ash was dead. She had ceased to exist. She had killed herself.

His life-giver. It was sad, endlessly sad. But he wasn't about to cry. He had work to do. His future with Una depended on him accomplishing it.

He labored vigorously that designated hour. Every step brought him closer to his goal of fencing off the Doreen-Ash area tightly and securely for all eternity. It wasn't a question of forgetting—and it is much harder to manipulate what surrounds the dead than the living. No memory is added after a person is dead; he or she reacts to nothing anymore, and exists in immutability. The one that Ástamama vanished into, with a single 'Yes' on her lips.

But it was possible to make memories harmless, as well as printed oddities about you; it was possible to fence them off, as you would a raging bull. Truth be told, the vicious bulls in the countryside were the only thing that had really frightened him back in the day—but now he was scared to death of their successor, Doreen Ash. He was going to take an hour to drive in fence poles around a dead woman who wouldn't lie still, and he worked hard at it, covered in sweat in the noonday sun on Long Island, so preoccupied that he was nearly hit by two cars, not just one.

Why had she done this? What drove her to it, just when a prospective bestseller had been published, now when she should have been enjoying the fruits of her labor over that book, when she should have been bathing herself in the light of success, as she had begun to do at the publication party? No one, not even a psychic, would have thought that she was on the verge of disappearing from the world. And how had she done so? He might possibly get some answers to that question in the media. But not as to why, and not as to why she did so precisely on the evening or the night after the book was published.

One thing, however, he thought he might know: when she decided to go through with it. A person who takes the step of parting from the world voluntarily must have considered it beforehand, but at a certain time there comes a point when there's no turning back. That point was when he said to her, at the publication party: *Never as much as today*—that she had never been as beautiful as that day—and she had repeated the words: *Never as much as today*, and smiled thoughtfully, as if she suddenly had an idea that she was going to keep to herself.

With ten minutes remaining of his hour-long run from Doreen Ash, it crossed Karl's mind to contact Liina Minuti, but after some time had passed. In exactly a month from now—and ask if he could come and talk to her. It would be easier for him to fence off Doreen Ash if he knew more about her—what sort of person she had been, in general—and about the end.

He went to the bakery on the corner, even if he wasn't in the habit of walking sweaty and half-naked into stores, and bought a number of freshly baked pastries as a late breakfast for Una. He walked the final steps home with his senses awash in the fragrance of baked goods and his mind full of Una. She was up and about, the dear, sitting in her strappy nightgown out on the bedroom balcony, having coffee. She had fixed herself a latte, from a masterwork of design that Karl had brought with him from Italy.

Una welcomed the man and the freshly-baked goods, particularly a warm marzipan croissant, which was her favorite pastry, and which she had been certain could not be gotten anywhere outside of Germany—until she moved into a house on Long Island that had been meant for her for so long.

At the Home of Doreen Ash

Karl Ástuson, who knew how to make plans and to follow up on them, held his course and wrote Liina Minuti a letter a month after Doreen died. He wrote and rejected eight drafts before sending the ninth. First, he offered his condolences. Then he stated that she had saved his life, and that he had not gotten to know this exceptionally important person as much as he would have wanted. Would Liina Minuti do him the huge favor of meeting him?

It was a nervous man who awaited a reply. A man who had doubts about his intentions. And gave no thought to the embarrassment of being exposed as The Good Lover himself, as stood in the inscribed copy that had been destroyed in two stages the evening before the author took her life.

Karl Ástuson relaxed immediately upon receiving a friendly letter from Liina Minuti. He no longer doubted his sanity, and hurried lightheartedly to Doreen Ash's address at the appointed time, with nineteen yellow roses. One noticeably bigger and more beautiful, like the roses from the petrol station bouquet that evening on Silfurströnd.

The psychologist Liina Minuti made things easy for Karl Ástuson. She was straightforward and cheerful, if anything—unlike the strict, composed Liina from the publication party. She hadn't even bothered to comb her hair in any noticeable way that day. A woman in a red, hippyish cotton tunic, barefoot, with black nail polish on her toenails.

The apartment that she and Doreen had shared was colorful and warm. Dainty, decorative furniture from China contrasted with an oversized sectional sofa, vacuous modern art and long shelves full of exotic little objects. The living room looked slightly chaotic, but it gave him a certain sense of security—or at least that's what the guest thought until he sat down in a corner of the sofa and felt as if he'd shrunk by several sizes.

Liina sat down at the opposite corner of the sofa. The distance between the two conversees on the same piece of furniture was so great that Karl Ástuson realized he wouldn't be able to speak in his usual quiet tones.

'I'm glad you came,' said the lady of the house. 'I have so few people to talk to about Doreen.'

'Thank you. It bothers me not knowing more about her—and this incomprehensible conclusion.' To his chagrin, Karl Ástuson, being unable to handle this unfamiliar key, ended his sentence in a falsetto tone.

'It wasn't incomprehensible,' said Liina, smiling.

A smile at such an inappropriate moment threw the guest off balance. He gave the frivolous mourner a stern look. And would not have been able to squeeze another word out of himself even if threatened with death.

Liina continued to smile despite her guest's stern look, and then said: 'Doreen spoke so much about you after you called from Iceland. You meant so much to her—"because she was able to make an impact on your life," she said. She said that you were the only person she'd actually been able to do something for in a way that mattered. That she'd been in a position to do so because she wasn't your doctor.'

'Being a psychiatrist isn't enviable.'

'Doreen was sick and tired of her practice. She felt that her patients were always stuck in the same rut, despite their increased insight. She actually didn't call them her patients, but 'her people.' "What's the use of this goddamn insight," she'd often say. "Since it doesn't change anything." Then she'd repeat a few of the typical complaints and ask: "How can they keep harping on about this after ten years of therapy?"'

'It must have been a relief for her to quit.'

'You can only imagine. But she was stuck with two patients—her "oddments"—or they with her. It was an emotional relationship, far beyond the bounds of all the rules. They got so much on her nerves that she said she had to take painkillers following their sessions. Mama's boys. Sucklers. And she allowed them to suckle. She said she wanted nothing more than to take them in her arms like big teddy bears and cuddle them. Because it was a human touch that they needed! Both homosexuals deep down, but didn't want to face it. She called them arch-homos. Her fingers itched to shove them out of their closets.'

Liina fell silent. Then she suddenly said, looking straight at Karl Ástuson as if it had something to do with him: 'She wanted to have a child.'

'Oh?'

'Yes. But she never said so out loud.'

'So how do you know, if she never said it?'

'Her oddments outed her. She mothered them like the worst mothersons. Robin and Markson were the little suckling babies she wanted, and they suckled at their fake mom's breast because she unbuttoned her shirt.'

These remarks directly echoed the clichés in *The Good Lover*. Unbelievable, the psychological claptrap that could well up from intelligent, highly-educated people. Karl said nothing and looked inquisitively at Liina.

But Liina was in her own world, and kept quiet for longer than the guest.

'Why on earth should she have kept it a secret if she wanted to have a child?' he finally asked.

'Out of fear that I would encourage her to go through with it.'

'What?'

'She realized that a child had no business in her life. But it didn't change the fact that she desperately wanted one. I'm sure it was her deepest wish.'

'Why did she want a child?' asked Karl, in such an astonished tone that Liina burst out laughing.

'The unlikeliest of people long to create families,' she then said. 'The most unlikely people. And it was Doreen's ardent desire to love unconditionally. But no one is in a position to do so but a mother.'

No one ... but a mother ...

If anyone had been loved unconditionally, it was Kalli Tyke, Karl Ástuson, the son of his mother. His mind drifted to the corner house with music—and he just managed to catch the tail-end of what Liina was saying: 'Doreen wouldn't have been a good mother, as she herself knew. It's even doubtful whether she was a good surrogate mother for her two oddments. I think they would have been better off somewhere else than with her. On the other hand, she managed to bring them together—after she was gone.'

'What sort of sorcery was that?'

'Robin and Markson met in the waiting room of Melanie van der Stein. There had been some mistake; two patients booked at the same time. They began chatting and Robin confided in Markson that his psychiatrist had killed herself, and recommended Melanie van der Stein instead. Well, there could hardly be many psychiatrists in New York that had recently killed themselves and recommended Melanie van der Stein instead. Doreen must have asked Melanie to schedule their appointments so that they would be sure to meet in the waiting room. She knew them well enough to know that they would make a great couple. She often spoke of it with me. What a shame it was that she wasn't permitted to bring them together. And provide them with the only thing they needed. Something she couldn't give them. A human touch. How I wish she could have known how it went.'

Karl Ástuson was transported back to the corner house with *The Farewell Waltz* and *Yes-tango*: *How I wish she could have known how it went.*

The undying sentence, when his mother was dead. She never got to know how it went with his high-school exams: how he graduated with first-class honors in math, determined to make up for how he'd earned only second-class honors in his class the year before—and that that was the last news she'd heard in her life.

What a shame that gymnastics should have weighed you down—the second-to-last words his mother had said.

Liina Minuti had stood up. Karl Ástuson thought he should be leaving, when she said: 'I'm going to show you the letters she sent them. You were such a favorite of hers that I'm sure she wouldn't have minded.'

'She made copies of the farewell letters she sent them?'

'She did. I don't really understand why. Unless it was for me to show them to you.'

'That can't be. Doreen wouldn't have suspected that I would visit you.'

'Doreen was often quite prescient.'

It was almost the same thing that Sigríður had said about Una: *nothing gets past Una.* The same might have been said about Sigríður Sherlock—that nothing got past her. And Lotta, as well. He was surrounded by women who were prescient, whom nothing could get past. From the very start—the others had nothing on Ástamama. She was so perceptive that her son didn't say much the first years of his life. He didn't have to; his mother knew immediately if he needed anything, or if anything were wrong.

The idea of reading letters that weren't meant for him made Karl Ástuson uncomfortable. Like snooping in a desk drawer. But he went through with it, and imagined that he was doing Doreen a belated favor.

Dear Robin,

Now we have come to a point that is not discussed in the manuals. I beg your forgiveness with all my heart, even if what I intend regarding you is inexcusable in your eyes. I am betraying your confidence, and in a certain sense, that is hardest of all. Also because it wasn't any less I who clung to you as you to me.

I am also sorry that I cannot explain to you how it came about that I no longer wish to live. In its own way, it is just too banal. If I had any sense of decency, I would be ashamed.

I implore you to find yourself a new psychiatrist, right away. I recommend Melanie van der Stein. Enclosed is her business card. I have prepared her. She knows about you, and will make arrangements to see you right away.

Lastly, I want to let you know that you are tremendously important to me, and made it easier for me to exist. I truly cherish you, and find you one of the sweetest, most interesting people that I've ever met. It is my hope, despite my letting you down so terribly now, that I have made some contribution to your living well.

Yours sincerely,
Doreen Ash

Hello, dear Markson,

I cannot help but write to you and ask for your forgiveness. You are the patient who has been with me the longest. There is only one other in my entire group that has meant as much to me as you have, far beyond all codes of ethics. I am ashamed of myself for giving up now, and I ask that you never dream of taking me as a role model. I know enough about you to know that you can live something called a life, and I beg you with all my heart to live it. Try to forget your unhappy psychiatrist, who could not help herself. I can wholeheartedly recommend Melanie van der Stein in my place. Enclosed is her business card; she knows about you. May good spirits watch over you.

Yours sincerely,
Doreen Ash

Karl Ástuson read these farewell letters from Doreen to her two oddments and said nothing, as suited her third oddment. Liina Minuti remained silent as well. This two-person silence sounded like a conspiracy; like the silence of a theater or a church.

'Shouldn't we have a gin and tonic in her memory?' asked the host suddenly, and Karl Ástuson realized that the long lack of refreshments breached the basic requirements of hospitality.

Liina Minuti went to the kitchen to mix their drinks, leaving her guest behind in his shadowy corner of the sofa. His head felt peculiar, which was normal. He had followed a dead woman to her home—she who had written an unprecedented book about him; a literary work that was also a completely absurd analysis of The Good Lover and his 'minx.' She called herself that in the book; his 'minx.' When he called her a lover. And what was he doing at her house? Her funeral had already taken place. Karl Ástuson could only shake his head.

Liina brought their gin and tonics, sat down next to him on the sofa, and they toasted the memory of Doreen Ash.

'How did you like the book?' asked Liina.

Karl Ástuson was unprepared for this obvious question. He was so furious with himself for being caught off guard that it drove him to answer as if he had smeared his tongue with olive oil: 'I'm ashamed to say it, but I mainly read thrillers and books on historical subjects. I'm not all that into novels, and this one is so unique that I've had trouble getting through it. Even if it is by a dear friend. But it's certainly a clever and original idea to combine literature and science like that.'

'I've wondered a great deal if Doreen was telling me the truth—whether she'd spun up a lie and pretended it was true. I have a feeling that it's as it looks: that The Good Lover is based on a real-life model.'

'She would have told you if there was a model, wouldn't she?'

'I'm not so sure of that.'

'She didn't exactly seem secretive.'

'She was and she wasn't. Something must have happened to her that changed her life. My guess is that it was a great love, exactly as it's described in the book.'

'Yes, but you are her great love.'

Liina laughed, in a cheerfully sarcastic tone: 'Please. Doreen is my love, the only one and then some, but it wasn't mutual.'

'There are so many kinds of love,' said Karl Ástuson. But then again, who was he to talk? He being a man who could only love one woman—apart from his mother.

'Perhaps. But a great love is constant; it never strays far.'

'It surprises me how well you're holding up.'

'I was prepared for it. I couldn't have known when, of course; but I knew how it would go, and that there would be nothing, absolutely nothing I could do to prevent it. Doreen was so determined that I couldn't have done anything. Yes, perhaps once or twice, but then she would have had to try again, and go through all the hassle. If I had kept constant watch over her, she would have been forced to do it all alone, far from me.'

'Why didn't she want to live?'

'I think she didn't want to exist apart from her great love. She couldn't settle for anything less than to live in it and with it. So she drank. Alcohol in that quantity is self-torture in its clearest form, and it is destructive. She would have had a chance if she'd stopped drinking. But she absolutely didn't want to, or couldn't. Doreen was a hyper realist. She saw how she would be in ten years, a drunk old biddy with a fleshy face and the shakes. That helped her to take the final step.'

'She had a little bar in her office,' said Karl Ástuson.

173

'I didn't know that. Did you go see her there more than once?'

'No, just that once. To thank her and give her the bracelet.'

'It went with her to the grave.'

'Oh?'

'She asked for it in her letter to me. But why did you have your name engraved in it?' Liina Minuti's tone was now a bit sharp, as if her guest had done something wrong.

'I can't explain it. Or, yes, to let her know how important she was to me—she fished me up when I called her, half-drowned. It's out of the question that I would have been able to swim ashore and make it to the woman next door if Doreen hadn't blown life back into me. It's thanks to her that I finally have something that I can call a life. I knew how it felt to be alive, because I'd tried it for a few months seventeen years ago. But in the meantime, I was hollow inside. I didn't even feel bad—any more than a dead person. I felt empty.'

'That's exactly what Doreen didn't want. I was a person of privilege. I loved. I love. I got to be with the one I loved. That can never be empty.'

Karl Ástuson was in his own world, thinking about emptiness caused by love and lovelessness, when Liina caught him by surprise with the question: 'Did you and Doreen ever sleep together?'

'Certainly not. We met just once—at a bar. Then we ate together, and she gave me her business card. Maybe she thought I needed a psychiatrist.'

'That's what she told me. I didn't believe it. I thought there'd been more. I suspected that you were The Good Lover from the book.'

'She used the bar as a prop; don't let that fool you.'

'I'm not fooled.'

'I think that novelists work much less with direct role

models then a lot of people think. They have more imagination than that—having to take things directly from reality.'

'He's similar in appearance to you—to say the least,' said Liina, aggressively.

'That's what I'm saying, novelists take details from reality to decorate their fiction.'

'That's true. Doreen had a good eye for decoration.' And Liina Minuti laughed.

Karl Ástuson smiled back and finished his drink. Now he looked straight into Liina's eyes and asked: 'How are you holding up so well?'

'I knew that I wouldn't have her with me for long. She hung in there until we'd finished *The Good Lover*; until we'd published the book. What I feared most was that she wouldn't last that long. Such a thing would have been a tremendous shock. I wouldn't have liked to live with it.'

'Have you come to terms with losing her?'

'It's not a question of coming to terms with it; it's a question of accepting the inevitable. I knew that my luck wouldn't last very long; not my tangible happiness. And Doreen prepared me a long time ago. She told me straight out over a year ago that she was going to give up. When the time came, she bade me farewell as beautifully as possible. We came home from the publishing party. We drank champagne; we made love for the last time. She said she loved me. That wasn't true, strictly speaking, yet I think it's nice that she said it, and she knew that I would appreciate it. I fell asleep. That's when she must have gone and taken her pills. Then she crawled back into bed with me. When I woke up, she was sleeping unusually deeply. I took her pulse and knew she was in a critical condition, and went and found what she had taken. Went back to the bed and took her in my arms. I sat with her like that until she passed. It took an hour and a half.'

Karl Ástuson bowed his head and wept. He pictured the woman staring at a bracelet with lapis lazuli stones as if she were trying to determine what time it was.

'It should really be me who's crying,' said Liina Minuti, handing the man a tissue.

'I'm sorry, I can't help myself.'

'There was nothing else to do but let her die in peace. That was what she wanted. It wasn't too much to ask for; strictly speaking, it wasn't up to me. And she was granted her wish— to die in peace in my arms. I don't think it would have been possible to save her even if I'd done anything. If she had been saved, she would have had to try again. And it would have been such a huge strain to try again. She'd prepared it in detail, chosen the right moment, after the publication party, after we'd made love. I had no business interfering with that plan.'

'What time did she pass away?'

'At half past ten in the morning.'

As Karl Ástuson skimmed quickly through the book about himself and Doreen Ash (most of the theoretical chapters would forever be a closed book to him, for example), its author was preparing her departure from the world, was drinking champagne with her lover. She had probably taken the pills as he was on the train home, extremely upset over what he'd read. As he was taking his long-awaited shower, before joining Una in bed, Doreen Ash cuddled up to the sleeping Liina Minuti and waited to lose consciousness, awaited death, patient and relieved. Probably frightened, as well. All who await death must be so, no matter how relieved they are—because no one knows of death except by word of mouth, and such report is unreliable.

She had never been closer to him, Doreen Ash, than right now, as he listened to this final news of her.

'This is so sad,' he said. And heard himself repeat the word: 'Sad.'

'Half past ten in the morning is a good time to die. The sun shone into her room at her final hour. I like to imagine that she sensed that final sun. She worshipped the sun. I know that that was how you met. There was no way she was going to sit inside the bar while the spring sun shone outside; and you came to her as she stood there on the sidewalk.'

'Yes.'

'And now you must forget her.'

'I'll forget her in my own way.'

'Take care not to fall in love with a dead woman.'

No risk of that, Karl Ástuson nearly said, before he remembered who he was talking to, and answered: 'I'll take care.'

'Don't let her take up too much space. She wouldn't have wanted that. You're building up a new life. The last thing she would have wanted was to get in your way. She proved that, for instance, by not writing you a farewell letter. Actually, I guess that you could regard *The Good Lover* as a public farewell letter to you.'

'That can't be.'

'Well, at least I have cause for quite some thought.'

'I can't forbid you to think. But you're barking up the wrong tree.'

'Something happened to her, which I think she was describing in the book. Something that changed her vision, something that caused her to get together with me. Of course, it wasn't the best of deals for me, but taking up with me was a kind of resignation on her part. The beginning of the end.'

'You can't say that.'

'Maybe not. I could just blame the alcohol. It poisoned her life, to the core. She was at the point where she had to start some days by forcing down shots, in between throwing up. It's horrible to watch the person you love torture herself like that. I couldn't do anything. Though of course I tried.'

'Hard to believe that you couldn't help her, with all your expertise and love.'

'Her unhappiness was stronger than all the world's love and knowledge.'

'I never saw her as an unhappy person.'

'A person's life force and brilliance can be deceptive.'

'Where did that unhappiness come from?'

'Unhappiness and misfortune are a mystery. Happiness is transparent.'

That statement had to be a proverb. He should have known from where. Was it Oriental?

Liina continued: 'Firstly, life didn't live up to her demands. Which was a strange thing for me to deal with. Not particularly uplifting, but I accepted it. That's why I helped her write this book, and to live on as she did so. She lived for this book. And I lived for Doreen, and the book along with her. Now I reap the reward: to witness our Good Lover grow and thrive with every new reader. I'm even going to become rich, too—moneywise. I get all the royalties. Doreen saw to that. Now, if I invest the money wisely, I might be able to live off of it even if I end up being a hundred, without ever having to lift a finger.'

'Congratulations.'

'Thanks,' said Liina, as she rose—just a bit quicker than could be considered professional for a psychologist at the conclusion of a session.

Karl Ástuson also stood up quickly, and heard himself say: 'I feel like I'm the third oddment. Maybe I should meet the other two?'

Liina laughed: 'Please, don't go bothering Robin and Markson. Take care of your own life. That's the best thing you could do for Doreen.'

'Yes, of course. No, that was a stupid idea.'

'Yes, it was. Don't let Doreen and her oddments take over your life. The woman is dead.'

'I know.'

'Thank you for coming. It did me good. I have almost no one to talk to about her. I've been tempted to give Robin and Markson a shout, but think it would be unprofessional. She's their therapist from beyond the grave and death, and in the worst case, I could ruin the progress they made with her and Melanie van der Stein.'

'Didn't you have any mutual friends that you could talk to?'

'Oh, they're so clueless that it would be worse than doing nothing. Her publisher is the worst. In love with her and devastated. He takes her suicide personally. As if he could have prevented it. Just think how bloody stupid people can be. And how badly he's handling it gets on my nerves. It's supposed to be me who's distraught.'

'That's true. I don't understand how you're holding up so well.'

'That's the third time you've said it.'

'All good things come in threes.'

Liina went quiet, before suddenly saying: 'You know, I've been granted more than my fair share. It's so rare to be able to be with your true love that it has to be categorized as a unique gift and privilege, even if conditions aren't exactly favorable to you. Think of what you've got. It hardly seems possible.'

'Without Doreen's intercession, it wouldn't have been possible. I don't understand it. I don't understand any of this. I suddenly found myself in the house next door to Una's, with a good friend of hers. An extremely nice person, but impossible to figure out. It was like meeting a ghost.'

'Doreen told me all about it. I'm used to incredible stories from work, but this one is totally unique. It will end with me visiting you at an old folks' home and hearing the whole tale all over again—and hopefully more.'

'You'll be welcome. I'll send for you.'

'No need. I'll come of my own accord.'

'May I kiss you goodbye?' asked Karl Ástuson, always the same darling son of his mother.

'Go ahead,' she said, pointing at her cheek. Something about this gesture reminded Karl Ástuson of Doreen Ash's dominance in bed.

'No need to blush,' said Liina Minuti.

Karl Ástuson put his arms around Doreen Ash's lover and kissed her firmly on the cheek.

'Goodbye,' he said. 'Thanks for giving me such a nice reception.'

'Thank you—yourself,' she said, before seeing him out.

The word echoed in Karl Ástuson's head all the way home to Long Island. *Yourself.* Although it wasn't exactly the same word that was written with black ink in his copy of *The Good Lover*, he could never shake his suspicion that Liina Minuti knew what Doreen had written in his copy and took advantage of her final opportunity to tease him.

A Song for Little Ears

The day they found out that Una was pregnant, Karl felt that the time had come to tell her a story she'd never heard. He hurried to the bakery to buy her a marzipan croissant and a bagel for himself, returned and set the table with Ástamama's fine coffee service (the same they'd used that breakup morning in August).

The afternoon sun illuminated a distant cluster of skyscrapers in the capital of the world, and Una relaxed in the glow of the same sun, her hair in the same short bob. She wore a pale-yellow embroidered silk shirt over Bermuda shorts, and crossed her bare legs.

Karl sat in the shade and looked at Una's tanned toes, with their white, iridescent toenails. Just then, they looked like ten pieces of candy, those toes that were so peculiarly dear to him ever since they were little girls' toes behind a screen, and he cleared his throat into his coffee mug and said that he was going to tell her a tale that was both old and new.

Once upon a time in Iceland, a boy named Karl and a girl named Una both went to Reykjavík High School, and they fell in love and became boyfriend and girlfriend, starting at the New Year's Eve bonfire down by the sea, where Karl had brought his little niece Ásta, all through the reading period for their final exams and up until Merchants' Weekend, when Una went with her friends to a music festival. She returned that Monday and broke up with Karl on Tuesday morning, at the kitchen table with coffee and a Swiss roll, very reticent and unusually pale (as if she were ill). Perhaps she had caught a cold at the festival.

Karl asked no questions, and with that, she was gone from the corner house forever. He was completely at a loss, and since losing his girlfriend was so terrible that even tears were made moot, he sat at the piano and played the Valse de l'adieu by Chopin, the same as he had played when a girl with short hair tried on velvet and lace in the same room, engendering Una Lara.

Karl could see his life clearly: he would never be able to love another woman, and was therefore doomed to be a bachelor; at such a young age. He wished he could die of sorrow on the spot, but since that was not an option, he would take a different, radical step and leave, as soon as possible, for New York. Mindful of his mother's advice that he should let his sister Fríða know straightaway if he ever thought of visiting that city, he called her. She immediately went to see her brother, who lived all alone in the corner house.

As was Fríða's habit, she got right to the point and said that their mother had entrusted her with the secret of Karl's paternity—and now he should know it too, since he was on his way to New York, where his father lived. By now he was an elderly man, and his name was Karol Ash, half Polish and half Native American. A married man, the father of two daughters, a strict Catholic. That is why their mother Ásta had not had the heart to reveal Karl's paternity. Karl, on the other hand, was permitted to contact his father according to established rules, through a lawyer.

Karl then said to his sister: 'My father has been lost to me for so long, without me missing him, that I don't feel any need to find him. And I will never have a child to tell who its grandfather was and what kind of a man he was, because Una dumped me *this morning. On the other hand, no one ever knows what life has in store for him. So, I'll go and try to meet my father, for this one single purpose: so that if, by some extremely unlikely chance, I ever have a descendant, he'll have some clue about his grandfather.'*

Fríða felt sorry for her half-brother and would have liked to comfort him, even though that would have been impossible, since he was inconsolable. She added, however, that she felt their mother hadn't been right in keeping Karl's paternity a secret; she really ought to have told him herself, long before her death.

'You can never really know other people,' Karl then said, his mind on how his one true love had broken up with him unexpectedly earlier that day, and added: 'You can't ever really know your own mother.'

'Least of all her,' said Fríða, and the half-siblings exchanged meaningful glances.

Now Karl and Fríða went to work and did what needed to be done to sell the corner house and share the profits equally. Several irreplaceable objects from the house were put into secure storage, such as the sewing machine and the beautiful old screen, which Karl had shipped over after he was better set financially. The piano and finely crafted dining-room furniture, among other things, went to Fríða, whereas the siblings divided the books between them, according to their mother's instructions.

To cut a long story short, the house was ready to put on the market the day that Karl Ástuson left Iceland for good, which was on the fourteenth of September, his birthday. That day, he turned twenty. On the fifteenth of September, his love, Una, turned twenty years old, but time had not allowed them to celebrate a single birthday together, even when only a few hours separated their birthdays. On the flight to New York, he shed silent tears over this.

After shedding tears a second time, in Grand Central Station,

*and then never again throughout his years of solitude, he imme-
diately contacted his father's lawyer. A meeting was arranged for
the following day, surprisingly enough in a hotel room, as if they
were lovers forced to meet on the sly, which made Karl realize as
never before what a secret his origin was.*

*Karol Ash was around seventy and looked like Almighty God,
with white hair and a beard. He even wore a big gold ring with a
red ruby on one of his fingers. He was a mild man, quick-witted
and with a sense of humor, but the meeting seemed to be difficult
for him, causing an upheaval of emotions and tears.*

*'The son I always wanted to have,' he blurted out. 'How happy
I am that you exist, and have so much potential.'*

It was a great relief to Karl not to be a disappointment to his
father, when it came down to it, but quite the opposite—and
ultimately, this was a good and meaningful thing to hold onto
throughout his life. It also meant a lot to him how proud his
father was of him—how fine-looking he was, skilled at playing
the piano, and more.

By this point in the story, Karol Ash was quite ill, and he said
that he didn't have much longer to live, but that he would make
things easier for Karl in terms of housing and other things, and
said that his lawyer would continue to do so after he was gone.
In addition, he presented Karl with an heirloom from his grandmother Anna: a necklace with garnets, and Karl cherished this
gift, even though he didn't know what to do with it.

This was the only time that Karl met his father, because shortly
afterward, the man's illness took such a foul turn that another
meeting was impossible. However, he did call and bid his son
farewell with the most beautiful of words, saying that he was a
blessing from heaven. Karol Ash died in early December.

Karl thought remarkably little about the life and death of Karol
Ash, having already written off the possibility of ever having a

father. Yet a feeling of emptiness did in fact take hold of his heart in the big city after his newfound father was gone—added to the emptiness he felt after the loss of Una and Ástamama.

And that is why I'm telling you this story now, Una. Both you and our child deserve to know its descent.

When Karl had finished telling Una this peculiar story out beneath the blessed sun, he went to the music room and took out a battered old suitcase. In it was a little girl's sweater, a score of the *Yes-tango* for piano, violin, clarinet, sewing machine, and soprano, and one of his math books from high school. He had written his name on the first page, in handwriting that hadn't changed. Below his name Una had written: *Te amo, Una.*

Karl lingered over these three objects: sweater, book and musical score, locked up together for seventeen years, causing magic to happen in the suitcase, magic that he conjured up by contemplating the suitcase's contents for hours at a time, particularly to the strains of Purcell's *Welcome Home* aria. So powerful was this method that everything had to give way before it, eventually—hocus pocus!, and two, soon to be three, would live happily ever after.

He took the sweater from the suitcase and shut it, and then put it back in its place with the *Yes-tango* and math book. The book would remain his secret. If he passed away before Una, which he earnestly hoped he would not do, she would find it; otherwise not. He had long since made written arrangements that the notebook would go with him to the grave. Lotta had seen to it that the document be appended to his will.

That had been a historical moment. Lotta had broken an unwritten rule and asked coldly what was so special about this math book.

The answer was straightforward: *Nothing, nothing but life as it is, is buried in this book.*

He could barely believe it, but now he was on his way out of the room, holding a little sweater, all the way out to the balcony. There he showed Una the sweater and told her the story, finally.

Only then did Una weep. Her tears fell onto the violet knitting, and she told her man, to whom she was not yet married, that she loved him, that she had never loved anyone but him, that she would always love him. At that, she began to sob in earnest, and still sobbed a bit when she said that she was going to take his name and go by Una Ástuson, even though she was generally against the foreign custom of women taking their husbands' names.

When she had calmed down enough to be able to finish her marzipan croissant, they continued to talk about family names, and given names, too. They agreed that if it was a girl, then Karl could choose her name, and if it was a boy, Una got to choose. That Sigríður at Silfurströnd 5 (whom Una called Aunt Sigríður) should be the child's godmother, unless she had quit traveling, as she had said.

The day that they found out that Una was carrying a girl, Karl Ástuson had to make a quick trip to New York. He started, according to plan, on the corner of 7th and 55th, where he had seen her at a distance, a woman alone on the sidewalk. It was an unexpected moment of sunlight on a cloudy day and he was transported back in time to when he met the midwife of his new life in a white wrap dress, and said to her: *There's no way I'm staying inside now that the sun is finally out.*

She: *I've been chasing after the sun since I can remember.*

He: *Just as well it wasn't rainbows.*

And she looked up, as if he'd said something poignant (that look wasn't included in the book *The Good Lover*, as its author hadn't seen her own expression) and hurriedly touched glasses

186

with him. (Their toast, however, held its place in the book.)

Later he heard that the sun worshipper, as she was, had gotten to die in peace in radiant morning sunshine.

His next stop was the flower shop where it would have been apt to buy flowers for Doreen Ash, even if it were only one rose, before they had dinner together. He had wanted to, but thought it too sentimental. For a second time, he failed to give her flowers—at the party for the publication of her book.

Now she was dead, and only then did she receive flowers. Twenty-five yellow roses. He had no idea whether Doreen Ash liked roses or the number twenty-five, even less whether she thought yellow was an ugly or beautiful color. He just couldn't think of anything else, but it matched this glorious time—a summer that was no longer a promise of something to come, but of something that had come and could not reach any higher. No more than his own life, his high-summer life with Una and the baby that was on its way. A baby girl, as a matter of fact, who would come into the world before the end of the year.

A child that Doreen Ash had wanted to have, and have with him, *himself*. He should have understood that when they spoke at her office. She had asked him directly about his feelings about having a child; she had then been thinking about the likelihood of his child's coming into existence—the child that she would not have with him.

The greatest wish of the unlikeliest of people is to create families, as Liina had said. But he had never wanted to create a family; he had wanted Una. It was as simple as that.

Now, finally, it crossed his mind that he might have been something of a happy man all those years without Una—because he was a lover. Much more that than empty inside, as he would have described himself. Did he then have to rewrite the story of his seventeen Una-less years from scratch? The years that he loved, more steadfast than the Pole star, the woman he never saw. Yet never lost sight of.

Immense pride swelled up inside Karl Ástuson. He was an accomplisher who had set a world record without even knowing it. An African runner from somewhere out in the bush, who was all decked up to participate in the Olympics and outran all the white marathon runners in the final sprint.

When he finally caught sight of a yellow cab, he decided not to take it to the cemetery. He was going to walk. It would take an hour, like his failed attempt to erect fence poles around the memory of Doreen Ash over a month ago. Then he had run as if the devil were on his tail. Now he walked slowly, deliberately pulling up the fence poles one after another. Doreen Ash was welcome around him. A welcome benefactress. He even found something appropriate to say, the New Year's Eve words as Ástamama had chanted them, addressing them instead to his good fairy:

Let those who wish to, come,
Let those who wish to, stay,
Without harm to me and mine,
Particularly my dear Doreen Ash.

She was one thing and another, that woman; more or less pleasant, even more or less pretty. But from now on, she would be one thing and one thing only for her storybook hero in the human world: a good fairy who had waved a magic wand and transformed him into a happy man. For that, he would remember her every day for the rest of his life. That was number one on the agenda concerning her—it would be easy. It would be much more difficult to eliminate a Good Lover, with guilt and all. Because he was guilty; he was inadvertently responsible for Doreen Ash's death. He was going to bear that guilt like a real man, not like some ridiculous character from a novel. Because that Good Lover didn't exist; it was an invention, a penalty paid for happiness, a sending from a woman who didn't exist either, any more than other writers, and it was his task to erase this caricature of himself. To do this, he could derive strength from two women, and the unborn one made all the difference.

Following Liina's precise directions, he found the grave right away. She had in fact said to him: 'Please, don't go and make habit of visiting Doreen's grave.' And he answered: 'I'll only go this one time.'

And that is what he intended to do. He had come for the first and last time to the tombstone with that name. The name of the woman named Ash, just like him, and therefore, could just as well have been his half-sister, but luckily, was not.

There he stood, Karl Ástuson *himself*, at the grave of his life-giver, hugging twenty-five giant roses that had started to droop a bit. For the moment, he couldn't determine the best way to unburden himself of them. He hadn't thought of a container. So be it. And he hadn't come here to think about roses, but to tell her one thing, the woman lying there, even if he didn't harbor much hope that she would hear.

It so happened that there was barely enough privacy in the place of peace itself to speak to those who were surrounded by the world's longest silence, because a silver-haired woman in a violet shirt was noisily planting a bush on the grave two over. She had just begun, forcing him to deliver his eulogy in her hearing.

He laid the roses on the grave. The buds touched the name on the tombstone and the stems rested in the shade of a big-leaved potted plant holding a bright red flower. Perhaps the roses' lives would be prolonged being beneath this plant—which seemed to be of the sort that Robin and Markson might have planted on the grave of their pseudo-mother—the one who longed for children and had taken two adult ones under her wing, rather than none.

He recalled Doreen's words: 'You strap your children with the burden of dying.' Unavoidably, what one old Icelandic book says is the hardest thing of all would also be her fate, his unborn little girl.

Ástamama had welcomed it with a single 'Yes.' It was a clear and bright yes, like what a young woman might say when she opens the front door, having put on her coat, and is heading out to run some errands. Perhaps just downtown, and is reminding herself of something that she mustn't forget.

Who knew—maybe in the future he would tell his grandchild about its grandmother's 'yes' just before she passed. In the future that was brimming with promise, finally; now that an actual child had settled there. A girl, no less. Who would have a rich father, the guardian of treasure in a magic suitcase: the *Yes-tango* and a math book—but the third part of the magic, the sweater itself, was already on the loose.

Of course he would perform the *Yes-tango* at one of his daughter's birthdays. Maybe when she turned eleven. Her mother could play the piano part, unless the birthday girl herself were good enough by then to do so. But he himself would have to see to the sewing machine. The same machine, luckily, that was used at the premier of the piece. His sister Fríða would be excellent as the soprano, since her voice was similar to Ástamama's, yet never more than an imitation of its silver.

And Karl Ástuson was certain that he would write a song for his child, as Ástamama had done for him, to prove to him that the world was not tuneless. He knew immediately what it would be called: *A Song for Little Ears*, and he listened to a melody that he was going to play often in Una's presence, because the mother's womb is not so isolated that the child can't sense some of what is going on outside it.

When the child had come into the world and was lying in its crib, naturally helpless, of course, following its separation from its mother, it would have the song as proof that it was welcome and always had been.

Karl Ástuson looked at his watch and saw that he had no more time for dawdling. He straightened his back, took a deep breath, and said out loud: 'Her name is going to be Ásta Doreen.'

The woman at the other grave looked up and nodded. Karl Ástuson nodded back, and in his mind went over the names that his daughter could choose from when she grew up: Ásta Doreen Karlsdóttir, Ásta Doreen Ástuson, Ásta Doreen Ash— and then prepared himself to come to grips with a new kind of happiness.

For more information, visit us at www.worldeditions.org.